Minot Judson Savage

Christianity the Science of Manhood

a book for questioners

Minot Judson Savage

Christianity the Science of Manhood
a book for questioners

ISBN/EAN: 9783337368975

Printed in Europe, USA, Canada, Australia, Japan

Cover: Foto ©Andreas Hilbeck / pixelio.de

More available books at **www.hansebooks.com**

CHRISTIANITY

THE

SCIENCE OF MANHOOD

A Book for Questioners

BY

MINOT JUDSON SAVAGE

BOSTON
GEO. H. ELLIS, PUBLISHER
101 MILK STREET
1880

Dedication.

---◆---

NOTE TO THE SECOND EDITION.

FROM the tone of *some* of the criticisms on the First Edition it seems desirable to make the following explanations, though I supposed the purpose of the book was made clear enough in its own development.

It is *not* to be taken as *all of my creed.* Neither does it claim to set forth the *whole of Christianity.* It *neither affirms nor denies* prophecy, miracles, inspiration, etc., etc. It follows one line of thought clear through, and purposely leaves one side the things that do not properly come within its intended scope.

Briefly, its main purpose is this: *to assume nothing that the most ultra unbeliever would care to question, and on that basis, to build up a valid argument for the practical acceptance of a living Christianity.*

I trusted that the use of such a brief and comprehensive argument would hardly need expounding. Evidences are " adequate " only when they meet the case. A Christianity, proved by miracles, is worthless to those who reject all miracles. The support of prophecy is of no value to those who do not accept the evangelical interpretations of prophecy. Historical evidence loses its effect on those whose faith is weak in the accuracy of all history, and the claim that the Bible history is inspired is an assumption of the whole matter, until the inspiration is satisfactorily proved. For these causes thousands reject any line of proof that *depends upon* or *even includes* these points. It was believed, therefore, that a service would be rendered *honest doubt* if a *reason for practical belief* could be given that *assumed nothing*.

All evidence is " inadequate " to the convincing of those who reject its premises.

PREFACE.

THIS small volume has been born of doubt and conflict. The author became a member of the Church at the age of thirteen. Since that time he has fought over the whole ground of modern skepticism, in a hand to hand contest with its shadows and its facts. He has found it impossible to rest in tradition, and has felt compelled to seek a reasonable basis on which to stand.

And there has been a stimulus to this conflict beyond his own personal longing for rest. He has tried to help others. And in so trying, has found the necessity of knowing a way that satisfied himself, along which he might point or pilot other pilgrim feet.

And he has not been content simply to

help those who were intellectually satisfied, and only needed an impulse to action. He has found great numbers who
took no steps, for the simple reason that
they were in doubt as to which way to
go; and he has learned that the ordinary
answers to skeptical questions were insuf-
ficient to convince skeptics, because they
failed to meet them on their own ground.

In the outline of thought that follows,
he has set forth what has seemed a solid
pathway to his own feet; and he only
hopes that it may have the feeling of
God's firm earth beneath the tread of
those that may choose to follow him.

If there is anything of worth in the
argument, its readers may give half the
credit to my brother, the Rev. W. H. Savage, who has helped me think it through.
The faults of execution may be wholly
charged on me.

Hannibal, Mo., *February*, 1873.

CONTENTS

PART I.

PRINCIPLES OF MANHOOD

PART II.

THEIR CORRELATE — CHRISTIANITY

PART III.

THE LESSON

PART IV.

SUGGESTIONS

CHRISTIANITY THE SCIENCE OF MANHOOD.

PRINCIPLES OF MANHOOD.

CHAPTER I.

FACTORS OF MANHOOD.

To find out what makes a true man, it is needful only to look at his parts and faculties, to conceive them completely developed, unperverted, rightly ranked, and set in harmonious relations with each other. All these are needful, and no more. If any wrong or evil exists, it must be for lack of one of these. Since, if any essential part of man as we find him is evil, then is God become the author of that evil, and human responsibility for it is gone.

Taking it for granted then, that they

are right, in their right development and use, let us see what kind of being the true man is, by looking at the different main elements that compose him.

First, and most obviously, man is a physical being, an animal. Like the great pyramid, though the summit of his being catch early and hold late the light of heaven, though the clouds hang round it and it seem to hold companionship with the stars, yet its base is in the dust. And being an animal he ought to be a perfect one.

This seems to be a natural and true conclusion; and yet, that it has not always appeared so, is evident from the strangely conflicting theories of the body that have obtained at different periods of the past At some times, and among some nations, matter has been deemed divine; physical symmetry, majesty, and beauty have been the highest types of the godlike; and heaven itself has been peopled with deities whose right to godhood has been hardly more than an undying physical perfection. And then, whole ages and civilizations have been characterized by the conception that the essence of evil itself was in matter, and that the pathway toward human perfection lay in the direction of bodily repression and extinction. Perhaps the age of Pericles in Greece may stand for the expression of the one theory, and that of Monasticism in Europe, of the other.

But both of these are at polar extremes from the truth. One cannot be true, if man is anything higher than animal. The other must be false, unless the forces of creation are at war with each other, or the supreme power is malign.

The body then is good. It is to be symmetrically developed and used. It is the shrine, vehicle, and instrument of the entire manhood. By means of it the man is set in relationships with the material world. And since through it the entire circle of human activities that make society, art, science, civilization, find their expression, and since the quality of the expression depends largely on the fitness of the instrument, the perfection of the physical life is an essential part of the perfect manhood.

But man is also an intellectual being. As such a being his end is truth. Perfection as a truth-seeker then is his perfection as an intellectual being. This requires that all his intellectual faculties be developed and trained to their utmost possible power.

Beside this power, the result of healthy training, there should be cultivated a rigid impartiality. A far-seeing eye is of little practical value, unless it sees things as they are. If right lines look crooked, if square surfaces appear round, if colors are blurred and changed, the wonderful keenness of vision only extends the range of the self-disordered chaos. Not opinions, not hopes, not fears, not wishes, but *truth* should be the one thing always and everywhere demanded by the healthful intellect. In its proper sphere, and following its proper methods, the intellect has no right to be anything but an inexorable logic machine. For since truth is the most difficult object of endeavor, it becomes sacred duty to hold the mind in equipoise for evidence only to influence. There are truths that do not come to us through the logical understanding, and that therefore the logical understanding has no right to condemn. But, in its legitimate field, the intellect has no right to be guided by anything but fact and evidence. It is morally binding on a man to doubt, so long as a thing that is knowable by the understanding, and is provable, remains unproven. But the minds of most men are decided, less than by almost anything else, by honestly-searched evidence. Like unfair balances, they turn in disregard of the weights; and, which-ever way they stand, indicate nothing of value.

The affectional nature is another essential factor of manhood. This it is that links him in community of interest with others, and makes him a social being.

Since the objects of his love must have a large reacting influence upon himself, it is of the utmost importance that he should train himself to love only the noblest and best. But as it is equally important that the love-faculty should be developed by its own exercise in order to the perfection of the whole man, as that the man himself should be benefited by the objects loved, his self-devotion should go out largely and freely toward all, of whatever nation, creed, class, or character. For the sunlight is not soiled by shining in the gutter. It ever manifests new phases of its own glory by glancing from pebbles and bits of broken glass. So the heart of man only becomes nobler and purer by raying out and down its sincere love on all that God has made.

The true object and inspiration of love is that which is lovable. The faculty can find exercise in the presence of nothing else. A sense of duty cannot produce love. Fear cannot produce it. Compulsion, in its presence, has no power. As well might duty or fear or compulsion drive the sense of smell, or make the ear find music in disagreeable sounds. The heart can thus find true scope for its largest exercise only in that which is perfect love.

Once more, man has always and everywhere manifested the presence and power of a religious faculty. However rudimentary, and under whatever grotesque form, this religious faculty makes itself apparent as a fact, and felt as a power. Perhaps no other force has so shaped society, so made and unmade governments, so dominated the world.

This religious faculty supposes a power or powers above man to which he owes allegiance. It recognizes this power as the arbiter of human destiny.

It also supposes the existence of an ultimate right and wrong; and makes these the law of moral action.

With a remarkable unanimity it has also linked with itself the expectation of a future life, and made the conditions immediately following this life hinge upon man's present career.

These, then, — the physical, intellectual, affectional, and religious, — are the important factors of manhood that our present purpose calls us to notice.

NOTE. — It is not claimed that this fourfold division of man has any scientific value. It is made merely for convenience' sake. The argument holds equally with any other division whatever; or with no division at all.

CHAPTER II.

BODY, mind, heart, spirit, — we have found that these all are factors of man as he actually exists. Or, to give it such expression as no one can deny, man sustains physical, mental, affectional, and religious relations. The faculties which make up his fitness for these relations constitute him what he is. But unless rightly combined and proportioned, they cannot make a true manhood, any more than roots and trunk and boughs and leaves make a tree, when the roots are in the air, and one of the boughs is larger than the trunk. Relation and proportion have as much to do with making men, as do the essential elements themselves. A man may have hands, and feet, and eyes, and nose, and ears, and each one of them, in itself considered, be perfect, and yet he be a monster.   Let one eye be twice as large as the other, his nose like an elephant's trunk, and the fingers of one hand be six inches in length; each of these might be as beautiful as the limbs of the Belviderian Apollo, but the beauty of parts would be lost in the monstrous disproportion.

The true manhood then demands not only all the parts of a man, and all these parts developed to individual perfection, but, with equal imperiousness, that they be in harmony of combination.

And one thing more, of no less importance, is their rank.   According as one or the other takes the headship, there result distinct classes of men, philosophies, and religions.   And where either one has a disproportionate growth, or a disproportionate control, the harmony of manhood is gone.   The past failures of the world are found just here.   It is a lack of equilibrium.

When the body assumes supremacy, there results the sensualist type. This is the grossest form of error. The man becomes metamorphosed, like the companions of Ulysses at Circe's palace, into swine. Not only is the religious nature degraded, but the intellect is warped, and the heart is deflowered. The whole man trails his glory in the mire of shame. This "psychical man," as Paul calls him, has been both the creator and the product of religions. He has made and corrupted philosophies. He has brought states and civilizations to the lowest depth of degradation that the world has ever seen.

Let the body then have the place that belongs to it; but do not adopt that style of architecture — which only the moral history of the world has been so absurdly base as to show a specimen of — that places the mud-sills above the cap-stone of the temple.

The intellect also may rule to the destruction of true manhood. He is worth very little who is not intellectual; but he who is all intellect is worth no more. The logical understanding has its place, and a very noble place it is. But in the true manhood it must not be permitted to usurp positions that it cannot, ought not to fill. If it deposes or dwarfs the affectional nature, it makes a man of a hard and unattractive type. He may be a good machine for working out certain forms of truth, but as a man, he is a poor specimen, and he is fitted to seek and find truth only in certain departments. If it presumes to dogmatize in spiritual matters, it may become only a guide to error. It is here beyond its range, as much as the eye would be in attempting to criticise a symphony.

The intellect has done marvels in its own proper sphere. Noble philosophies and wondrous sciences has it constructed. But out of its sphere, it is like the hand dictating and dogmatizing about the mountain tops and the stars.

Those characters in which the affections predominate over the other factors of manhood are not so common, or at any rate not so striking and noticeable, as are the other types. But the kind of manhood produced by it is still partial and incomplete. It is not degraded like sensualism. It is not hard or arrogant like intellectualism. It is rather partial and weak, doing injustice, not purposely and with forethought, but through a moral inability to hold by the right against the current of the impulses and inclinations.

The heart indeed, in one sense, ought to rule. But it should rule through a clear intellectual perception of, and a constant devotion to, right. It is when, ignoring this, it assumes to control in the interest of some subordinate object of affection, that the man is distorted and degraded from his proper rank, as one fitted for alliance with the highest.

The type of man that is formed by the enthusiastic exaltation of the religious faculty, to the prejudice and disregard of the other factors of manhood, is, in some respects, worse than any of the others. Wielding the most awful motives, it has a tremendous power of control. Despising and degrading the physical, it cuts loose from the anchorage of facts. Disdaining the guidance of the rudder, reason, and blinking the headland lights of history, it sails a Flying-Dutchman cruise, starting from no certain port, and aiming at no certain haven. Mistaking the cloud-shapes of twilight, or the flitting forms of fancy, for the facts and beings of a real world, it steers toward no-man's-land, and anchors to a fog-bank. Crushing out the heart, in obedience to what it deems the fiat of Heaven, it becomes cruel and inhuman.

A Pharisee, he thinks to preëmpt heaven, and despises others. A bigot, he merits and gets the contempt of the liberal. A fanatic, he anathematizes as heretics all who cannot look through his spectacles. A traditioner, he was born to his beliefs and interpretations, and he calmly ignores facts, until science and progress trip him up with them. And even then, he looks upon them as impertinences, and wonders that God should ever have made anything that will not fit into his system.

The true manhood then is not found in the dominion of any one of these to the ignoring or degrading of another. It is in the right development and ranking of them all. Man should be a pyramid, having his body for the base, and his religious faculty for the apex, with heart and brain between.

The body must be governed by the reason. The reason also must check and guide the action of heart and spirit, though they both are superior to it in their highest range and uses. A whole body, a clear, strong, quick intellect, a heart that loves the best, and an upward looking of the whole being to the absolute right and true, — these make a man all that it is possible for him to become.

CHAPTER III.

THE RELIGIOUS THE DISTINCTIVE FACTOR.

WHATEVER else or more man may be, he is an animal; and as we trace the upward grades of life we find him at the summit. By virtue of the fact that he includes in himself and completes all the forms of life below him, he takes precedence of all. But the fact of his animality is not that about which we are concerned; we wish to know whether he is anything more.

If we leave one side the religious faculty, we find him distinguished from those below him, not as different in kind, but only as higher in degree. That is, he has no new faculties superadded to those which he possesses in common with the animal, but only the animal faculties more

2

highly developed. The animal thinks, remembers, imagines, reasons, hopes, fears.
Man's capacity in all these directions is
simply more. The only thing that is
even an apparent exception to this statement is the fact, that man is capable of
conceiving and giving utterance to abstract ideas; while, so far as we know, the
animal is not. For instance, the dog
readily distinguishes between a round object and a square one, or between something that is red and another that is
black. But we have no evidence that he
has any idea of squareness or roundness,
or redness or blackness, apart from the
objects that manifest these qualities. But
this power of abstraction is not something
different in kind, so much as it is a higher
degree of the intellectual power.

The physical, the intellectual, and the
affectional natures, then, man shares with
the animal world. And before he can be
satisfactorily shown to be anything more

than a higher kind of animal, some other side of his nature must be found that shall set him in a whole new world of relationships. Is there anything about him that transcends these, and lifts him up to the level of a higher range of life? Let us see.

There are two ways of pursuing this inquiry, — the historical and the metaphysical. Glance at both.

If there is any other faculty in man, it will have found expression in his history. Has there been any such expression? In every land, and in all time, there are discoverable traces of the universal fact that man is a worshipper. Through fetish of stick or stone, through Ephesian temple, through Christian church, — whatever may be the medium, — the fear, or reverence, or love for a higher power has found expression. No race has yet been discovered where this sentiment of worship has been proved to be absent. There is nothing that can be regarded as even a remote parallel to this in any province of the animal kingdom.

Take now the metaphysical road to the same result. Can we trace any internal peculiarity of nature that can account for the outward manifestation ? After a com- parison of faculties, we find that man has a conscience. The distinguishing feature of this faculty is its perception of the fact of an ultimate and necessary right and wrong. There is no evidence that any other animal possesses this. The dog evinces a desire to please his master; and shows fear or shame at his displeasure. But we have no reason to suppose that he connects with these emotions any sense of moral well or ill desert. But the con- science of man compels him to think of right and wrong, apart from any will or personality whatever.

This possession of the religious faculty, then, differences man from all forms and kinds of animal life, not simply as higher in degree, but as separate in kind. It makes no difference whether you conceive him as created outright what he is to-day, or whether you think him evolved from the orders of life below him. Not where he came from, or how he came, but what he is, concerns us. He is, then, and always has been, a religious being. And since this religious faculty has always existed, and has always manifested itself in man, it is as unscientific to deny or blink the fact, as it would be to say he is not an intellectual animal. The same process of reasoning that eliminates the religious factor of manhood would, at the same time, do away with any other part of humanity whatever. That is not science which denies facts, but that which accepts and accounts for them.

Indeed, so far from its being a question as to whether the religious faculty is any essential and permanent factor of manhood, it is a truth easy of proof that it is the essential factor. There is no manhood without it. Take it away, and you relegate humanity to a permanent place among the brutes, and nothing can extricate it. All other things he shares with the life beneath him. If he is to emerge and take permanent rank as a being higher than animal, it must be by virtue of his religious nature. For, as was just said, this is the one thing which he has that the animal has not. Take this away and the manhood is gone.

For man thus to assume and assert his true place and rank in nature, it is absolutely essential that he cultivate and develop the religious side of his being. The only way for a fruit-bearing tree to assert its superiority over an unfruitful one is by bearing. As a shade tree, or for any other purpose, it may not be so good. So man is of value above and beyond the other animals, not by virtue of what he possesses in common with them, but because of what he is of more and higher than they.

And that he may be the highest kind of man, it is necessary that this faculty be rightly cultured and developed. Since it is an integral part of human nature, it will have some kind of expression. What kind then will determine what kind of a man. For this conscience is no infallible guide as to what is right or wrong, but only the faculty that asserts their necessary existence, and demands the submission of the whole being to what is seen to be right. For settling questions of casuistry, the determination of what is right or wrong in particular cases, there is needed all that goes to make up the enlightenment of the world. This is apparent from the fact, that even yet, in the most civilized countries, there is no complete agreement as to what is right on all special points. But among all, cultured or uncultured, the conscience equally speaks, commanding obedience to what each one believes to be right. A complete moral harmony of belief and action will have been attained only when all men have agreed as to what is the true religion and the true manhood.

NOTE. — For a scientific recognition of the points made in this chapter — a recognition which I came across since writing it — the reader is referred to the first of a series of articles on " The Natural History of Man," by Prof. A. Du Quatrefages, in the first number of the *Popular Science Monthly*, p. 63.

Also, to an article on " The Consciousness of Dogs," in one of the numbers of *The British Quarterly Review* for 1872.

CHAPTER IV.

RELIGION AS SEPARATED FROM MANHOOD

To say that a man cannot be truly religious without being a true man, and that he cannot be a true man without being truly religious, seems like the statement of a truism. And yet so far from its having been, or being now an accepted axiom, it would seem to be true that the great majority of religionists have never thought of it. Through the longer portion of history, and by the larger part of the people of the world, religion has not been considered an essential of manhood. Human life has been thought to be complete in its simple worldly relationships; and if above and beyond this any one has been specially devoted to the gods, he has been thought to have attained something

extra or super-human. God has been regarded as an external king; but as the
inmost spring and spirit of human character, He has not been in the thought of
men.

As the natural result of these ideas, religion has been something, not to inform
and develop the true life of humanity,
but merely a pathway to some special
favor of a distant heaven. Altars have
been reared to avert judgments. Rites
have been celebrated to ward off calami-
ties. Prayers and sacrifices have been
methods by which to tire, tease, or cajole
the gods into compliance with human
wishes. If men have been pious, they
have not been better as men; if impious,
not the worse.

More than this. Not only have religion
and manhood been separated, but frequently even religion and morality. At
some periods of the past it has been almost necessary to be irreligious — accord-

ing to the prevailing conceptions of religion — in order to be moral. Piety has been only a diplomatic contrivance by which to deal with the superior and dreaded powers of Heaven.

And, as a general statement, it is safe to say that, not only has this been, but it still is, the prevailing conception in most of the nations of the world. Practically, also, it governs the masses of Christendom. Particularly is this true of the hierarchical and ritualistic systems; and yet it is by no means confined to them. Church forms and sanctions, once supposed to be essential to character, at last come to usurp the place of character; and men are good Christians who are anything but good men.

To this fact have been due many of the revolts of men against nominal Christianity. And these revolts have been justifiable; for unbelief is better than belief of what is false. Voltaire's infidelity is better than the Christianity of Charles IX. of the St. Bartholomew. As Lord Bacon teaches, atheism is better than superstition.

This separation of religion and manhood colors the thinking and shapes the acting of the majority of the men and women of to-day. When they think of religion as the "one thing needful," it is not that it is needful to the true life here or hereafter; but needful to curry favor with an offended deity, or as a passport to a future heaven. It is not something essential to the plan of the life, but an addition, for the sake of certain extraneous advantages; and were there no thunder-storms to come for which this lightning-rod were needed, it were an outright inconvenience hardly to be borne.

To see how true this is, and in order to a clear understanding of the importance of being right just here, it will be well for us to glance at some of the prominent forms of Christianity that drop out of sight the manhood. Then we will pass to a view of the necessary identity of religion and manhood as rightly understood.

It is still true that the larger part of nominal Christians conceive religion to be simple churchism. The passport to God's favor in this life, and to heaven in the next, is only membership in an organization; and this membership is maintained not on the ground of character or good behavior. It is hardly apparent that it even has a tendency to produce these. The Church is supposed to have a monopoly of God's gifts and graces, and to bestow them on whomsoever she will, — as though Heaven had farmed out the world to the Church. So long as one yields unquestioning obedience, all is well. An Italian brigand can be pious, and not leave his profession, quite as well as a bishop. Plunder and prayer are not supposed to be incompatible. So far does this matter go, that the Church becomes an institution for covering, instead of delivering from sin.

Close akin to this, and yet differing in some cases, is sacramentalism. By this, I mean salvation by sacraments. Just after Lincoln's assassination, I was riding in the cars with a California clergyman, when he expressed grave doubts as to the dead President's future. And these doubts were grounded, not on a question as to his life or character, but only on the fact that he had not been baptized. Noble life, service of his kind, these weighed nothing against the damning fact that priestly, dripping finger tips had not touched his forehead. God's eternal love and life, or his eternal hate and punishment, are made to depend on a five-minute ceremony, that may or may not touch the manhood for better or for worse.

Another thing often supposed to be superior to manhood is orthodoxy. Intellectual belief is not unimportant. It may

make the man. But when crooked heads
and straight lives, and straight heads and
crooked lives are seen together, it becomes
apparent that this is not the essential of a
true life. Belief can be said to be essential only when by it is meant the practical
persuasion of the whole man. Epictetus
the Stoic Atheist, Spinoza the Pantheist,
Channing the Unitarian, these may show
the true manhood; while those who rest
in orthodoxy of belief may entirely miss
the way. For one who regards the words
of the Christ, there should be a better
reason for rejecting a man than " because
he followeth not with us."

Again, many rest in what, for want of
a better name, may be called conver-
sionism. Conversion, if it mean a change
from a bad life to a good one, is well.
But it is the true life, and not the turn-
ing-point, that is to be insisted on. I find
men thinking that religion means, not a
true life for God and their fellows, but that
they were once converted. But if one be

travelling in a wrong direction, it matters little that he has a certificate in his pocket attesting the fact that he once started right. If a man leads me up to a Canada thistle, and tells me that last year it was changed into a pear-tree, he will hardly expect me to prick my fingers on it trying to gather pears. Not what a man once became, but what he is now. If I find a pleasant day, I need no one to testify to the fact that there has been a sunrise. But talk not of a certain dawn, while it is still black as midnight. Let me see a true man, and I know he became such. If he be not one now, it matters little what he once was.

These then will suffice for illustrations to what an extent, even yet, the true religion is conceived as something apart from the true manhood.

NOTE. — What is here asserted of many forms of Christianity, so called, is wellnigh universally true of all other religions the wide world over. No one of them has, as its objective aim, a true manhood.

CHAPTER V.

TRUE RELIGION AND TRUE MANHOOD IDENTICAL.

WE have heretofore spoken popularly of the religious side of man's nature. Let it not be supposed, however, — except for purposes of analysis and discussion, — that it is intended to mark this off as a separate and distinct department of his being, any more than there is a division in the mind between that which thinks and that which remembers. If the law of right, which finds its exponent in the conscience, be anything, it is the regnant force of the whole man. There is no province of his being from which it can be excluded, or over which it does not claim to rule. He must be right, righteous — that is, truly religious — in body, mind,

3

and heart, quite as much as in his spiritual nature. The truly religious man, then, is simply he who is right in his whole manhood; and this is only to be a true man.

To bring this out clearly let us look at it from some of its different sides.

In the first place, note that the religious life is the natural activity and outcome of the essential manly faculty. We have seen already — in Chapter III. — that the religious is the distinctive factor of manhood. The natural activity and expression of this factor then can be only the true life and natural activity of the man. The true religious life and the true manly life are seen to be one.

Again, the truly religious life means simply the truly right life; and this truly right life can be nothing else than such a life as your being fits you for — a manly life, one lived after the highest manly ideal.

Once more, if you conceive a personal creator — no matter now whether you accept the popular or the Darwinian process in creation — you must think of him as having in mind an ideal of the not yet created man, and this ideal must include all that he can ever become. It must include all parts of him rightly developed, and rightly adjusted to his surroundings. As he exists in this ideal, he is no more than a perfect man, and he is no less than perfectly religious. The perfect manhood includes his right relations to his creator and his fellows; and this right relation means only that he is perfectly religious — *i. e.,* righteous. So the perfect manhood and the perfect religiousness are interchangeable terms.

From such a true manhood as we have imagined you cannot take away the religion as though it were an attribute or faculty; it is the principle of his organization, the plan of his structure, the law

of his life. As well might you take down
the entire plan of a house, and leave the
house itself still standing. The plan is
not the timber, the brick, or the stone ;
but it is the idea in accordance with which
every timber and brick and stone is put
and held in its place. So the true religiousness of a man is the plan of his whole
being, the idea of his organization. It
cannot be subtracted from it without tear-
ing the manhood down.

Religion is not something which manhood can get, or that can be added to it.
There is much loose, popular talk and
writing about " getting " religion. It is
not a distinct entity outside of a man to
be gotten. It is something to be — the
rightness of the manhood. The right
manhood then is necessarily religious;
and any manhood that is not religious is
not right.

Look at it from still another side.
Think of man as fallen, and rising toward

what he ought to be; or as undeveloped, and rising toward what he ought to be, — and in either case, he is only growing toward his perfect ideal. When he gets there, he will be only truly religious, righteous, right; and he will be such in virtue of the fact that he has come to be a perfect man.

And yet again, if a man is what God made him to be, — right in himself, right in relation to his fellows, right in his relation to God, — religion cannot make him any more or any better. This rightness is religion.

And lastly, if he is not thus right, the highest, and the only true work of religion must be to make him such. And when the work of religion is complete, and it has brought the manhood to what it ought to be, it has only succeeded in making the perfect man.

Thus from all these points of outlook the same great truth appears, — the true religion and the true manhood are identical. The religion is something so fundamental that there can be no true manhood without it. The perfectly religious man is only what he was made to be. And he who fails in this fails in the very first and highest essential of being a man. He is something one side of, and less than, what he was made for.

An irreligious man is a failure, just as a mowing machine is a failure when it will not mow, — no matter what else it does. No matter how beautiful its make. No matter how high its finish, nor how bright its painted decorations. It was made for a distinct and special purpose; if it fails in that, it fails of being a true mowing machine. So a man may be whatever else he will, if he fails of being what he was made to be, just in so far he comes short of being a man.

CHAPTER VI.

RIGHT ADJUSTMENT TO THE PRESENT.

THE architect, in deciding upon the plan of a building, takes into account not merely the materials and proportions of the structure, but also, as of no less importance, the site and the surroundings. The position being chosen with care, the house must then be adapted to the other houses or features of the landscape that are to become parts of the complete effect. The central figure on the painter's canvas is perfect only in relation to the general grouping and detail. The lady not only selects a fair flower for her bosom, but she also regards harmony of color and arrangement of parts. That man is not perfect who is so in and for himself alone. An essential part of true manhood is in

the relationships he sustains to other beings, in the midst of whom and with refer-
ence to whom his life is lived.

Humanity is not perfect when all its
units are perfect, if they are perfect simply as units. Perfect trunk, perfect limbs,
perfect twigs, perfect leaves, — all these
do not make a tree, if their perfection is
isolated and disjoined. It requires, besides
these, a perfect organization, according to
the law of an inward life, before that perfect whole, which we call a tree, stands
before us. And no artificial joining will
suffice. The workman may do his part
so well that the illusion shall be complete,
and yet the result is no more a tree than
the pile of fragments from which the sem-
blance was constructed. There is a soli-
darity of humanity which makes each
part perfect only as perfectly related to
every other part.

The history of the world so far is just
the history of human experiments in the

adjustment of these relations. When this adjustment shall have been attained, the problems of sociology and government will have been solved. The day of this complete adjustment may be very far away ; but the principles of the adjustment, and what the life shall be when so adjusted, it may not be very difficult to imagine. The secret can reside in nothing else than what we call the brotherhood of the race. When manhood is recognized as the basis of rights and duties, and all things work from and by and for this, then will the race be complete. The true social life of the present then must be that which works toward this ideal.

This principle of brotherhood will regulate the relations of inferiors to superiors.

This relationship is one of accidents, and not of essentials. Instead then of finding these distinctions occasions for envy, or stimulants to unhuman competition, a truer thought will seek the basis of brotherhood by striking down through them to the invariable characteristics of humanity. It will not teach the low to be content in abjectness, but will reveal to them something in themselves of higher dignity than condition. It will rebuke the tendency both to rebellion and self-contempt, and will show the lowly how to make those above them both teachers and shelter.

This brotherhood will also give the law to the other side of this relation, — that of superiors to inferiors.

Man is not great, nor rich, nor strong, for himself alone. He is not then to make these occasions for lording it over his fellows. The poor, the ignorant, the low, are not stepping-stones, nor lawful plunder; they are brothers to be respected and helped. He must use the advantage of his high position as a means of lifting up those beneath him. He is bound to help the weak by as much as he is stronger than they. He is bound to teach the ignorant by as much as he is wiser than they. His debt to all men is limited only by his superiority to them. Paul saw the law, when he wrote, "I am debtor both to the Greeks and to the Barbarians, both to the wise and to the unwise."

This principle also defines the relations of equals. Strictly speaking, there are no equals, while in another sense, all are equals. There is no one who has not some need that another may fill. "No man liveth to himself, and no man dieth to himself." Humanity is not a forest in which every tree is distinct. It is rather a banyan, all whose seemingly separate trunks are linked together in one common root beneath the soil, and braced above by arms that throb with a common life. Just so are men who call themselves independent and equal bound together in community of interest and hopes. He who holds himself aloof from the rest defrauds both himself and them. With hands clasped, with hearts keeping time, shoulder to shoulder, a band of brothers, they should march on to the " good time coming."

Such is the social brotherhood for which men hope in the hours of their highest inspiration.

This principle of brotherhood defines the first duty of governments.

It is evident that when the perfect manhood is attained all necessity for government will have passed by. Men may then do " what is right in their own eyes," because that will be the absolute right. The highest duty of governments then is to make themselves useless. That is, they are to do all they can to train men into such a state of self-government and social equipoise that they shall be no longer needed. It is the duty of the teacher to instruct his pupil up to his own level. When that is attained the teacher is useless, and the two are equals.

The law of progress then is towards democracy. Not that all men are ready for it yet. Not all students are ready to go out independently into the world. But it is not less true for that, that the true end of all schooling, from its primary department to the university, is to fit them for such graduation.

It will be apparent from our discussion, that social and governmental perfection can consist only in the perfect independency and brotherhood of individuals. That which perfects the individual then will perfect the race. The law is one, and its direction the same. There must be some one force of development and growth in accordance with, and through which, the completed manhood shall come. We see the goal afar off, and recognize something of what it shall be when attained. But the problem is to discover whence springs the breeze that shall fill the waiting sails, and hasten the ranked and orderly squadron across the turbulent present to the azure calm of that distant " sea of glass."

CHAPTER VII.

ONE more adjustment is needed in any complete scheme of human life ; and that is, adjustment to a possible future. No plan is perfect that leaves out of view any important contingency. Now whether or not there be any such proof of a future life as demands the assent of all reasonable minds, it is at least clear that such a future is possible. No one can be called irrational for believing it. And it is self-evident that, if there be a life to come, fitness for an advantageous entering upon it is of so much moment as to entitle it to take a leading rank in our attention.

It is not proposed here to enter upon any proof of immortality. So universal has been the faith that perhaps it is entitled to rank among the intuitive beliefs of mankind. At any rate it is so probable that no wise man is justified in leaving it out of his account. This life should be so lived as to make it the best possible preparation for an upward step in the next, if there be a next.

Its bare statement will make it apparent that he who is the completest man will be the best fitted to meet any possible future, or start out on any possible career that may await him. No matter what station or kind of life may be before him, that college graduate is fittest for it who is the most completely and symmetrically trained .in all his faculties and powers. Let him make the most of himself then on every side of his nature. Let him train, like an athlete, for every contingency. Thought, memory, imagination, every part should be fully developed; and then, in whatever direction he is called to act, he will be ready. So when one graduates from this life into an unknown other. Since he knows not definitely the conditions of that life, he should make himself ready for any. And this he will do by making himself the completest and best in every direction. He should seek to "come unto a perfect man;" and thus complete, he should stand before the veil that drops from sky to earth on the farther verge of life. And then, when the veil is lifted, there can be for him no surprise, no condemnation. He will be ready for any fate. To him there can come no evil. His ear will be quick to catch the sound of any voice that invites him higher; his hands will be ready to grasp any grander good; and his feet will be ready to climb.

This cannot be true of any one who trusts to anything else. Any special philosopher or religionist may be ready for his future, provided it is that which he imagines, and for which he builds his preparation. But if his fitness hang on

4

this supposition or that, he is ready for no other, and has but his one chance of success among many of failure. But he who through love and service of the best develops into the true and complete manhood — or who, as best he may, grows toward this — must be ready for any future over which a good being rules. He has all chances for success, and none for failure.

It is apparent then that whatever principle of adjustment may be found for the harmonizing and perfection of this life — for making the true manhood — will equally prove the principle of adjustment for the future.

PART II.

THEIR CORRELATE — CHRISTIANITY.

CHAPTER I.

CHRISTIANITY THE TRUE MANHOOD.

OUR next step ahead leads us to an investigation of the essential, formative principle of Christianity, to find out whether its complete working may be expected to issue in a complete humanity. If it fails this test, it must fall. If it endures it, no other thing can ever invalidate its claims; for it will thereby be proved accurately and perfectly to embody the true ideal of humanity.

There is no question that the present drift of the world's thinking is towards evolution in all things, as opposed to outside, mechanical contrivance and construction. The carpenter theory of the universe is giving way to the growth theory. Things evolve from within, in accordance with implanted seed-forms and plans, instead of being built and shaped from without. The whole tendency of modern science is in this direction. It does not touch the question of the divine original, or the proper creation of things, but only asks how and by what methods.

If this tendency of things be in the right direction — and I believe it to be — then we are justified in assuming that the true religion must consist in some one central, vital force, that may seize humanity at its centre, and work in it a formative force of development. For instance, it must be like the germ-force of a tree, that determines to what it shall grow. You cannot prune, or mould by outside pressure, an ash-tree into an oak. The germ determines its nature. The process of growth is only the unfolding of its central idea.

And so we may expect to find the true religion, not an institution pressing and shaping humanity from without, but a principle, a force germinant and expansive, determining the external form by the power of the inner life.

Does Christianity consist essentially in any such central principle and power of vital growth? And if so, will this power of growth develop the perfect manhood?

The founder of Christianity knew what He meant it to be, better than any of his followers, interpreters, or commentators. And he has condensed it into a phrase, — *Love to God and man is Christianity.* Not institutions, not successions, not sacraments, not faiths, not works, but love. "He that loveth is born of God," — is a Christian. He that loveth not is not a Christian. This statement from the lips of its founder precedes and outweighs all others, from whatever source. Any other claim or statement must be interpreted in the light of this. All other things are of value only as they help produce this. If they hinder it they are antichrist.

Christianity then is love; and it must stand or fall by this. Let us now trace out this life-force of the religion, and see in what it will result.

First, it will tend to develop the individual perfectly as an animal, but not chiefly for animal ends. And the explanation of this necessary tendency in Christianity is simply this. Love for the highest and best demands that the person governed by it become the most and best possible, in every direction, for the sake of others; and it absolutely and forever condemns any departure from this. Man then, whatever else and more he may be, being an animal, love commands to become the best and noblest and completest animal that the limits of his nature will allow.

It will tend toward this. Not that it

commonly, or even frequently attains it now. But this in no way invalidates the position. It takes the individual not only incomplete, but weighted down by ages of inherited evil. Its current flows into a stream already brackish and impure ; and at the point of junction its influence may be hardly seen. What it can do will be seen later down, when its volume has become predominant, and the sediment has been precipitated. In its practical working among men, it has also been subject to their misconceptions. The human mind being what it is, there is nothing more strange in their misconceiving and perverting their religion, than in their failing to get a correct theory of light. From these misconceptions have arisen ascetic and monastic perversions of the true use of the body. But in the light of experience and a broader study of social and political relations, these mistakes have appeared and been abandoned. And now no enlightened Christian thinks he can please God by abusing his body, or that the way to heaven is over the broken wrecks of physical laws. The body is coming to be recognized as the work of God, " fearfully and wonderfully made." Nothing in it is wrong, nothing superfluous. It is to be kept, ruled, and used, in accordance with the highest ideals and ends of humanity.

I said the body is not to be used chiefly for animal ends. Why not drop out the word chiefly, and say, the Christian is not to make the body the end of his action in any sense ? Because the body is an end, and a good end in itself. Only, not being the highest, it must always give way in the presence of what is more important. But when nothing more important is present, the body, its wants and desires, are an end in themselves. And this end may rightly be sought within the limits of the body's own natural and healthful laws. A man may smell a rose for the gratification of the sense of smell. He may rejoice in a sweet simply because it is sweet. He may hear music for the delight of the ear. Self-denial is a virtue only in view of an adequate cause.

But let a man make his body his chief end, that is, become animalized, and he not only casts off the bonds that ought to bind him in community of welfare to his fellows, and degrades himself below the proper level of his own true nature, but he also defeats his own animal welfare and happiness. The largest amount of sensuous happiness even is to be found in the proper and healthful, that is, lawful use of the powers and propensities of the body; just as the most and sweetest music comes not from abuse and breakage of the piano, but from care, and skillful playing. And as this proper use of the body is to give way only in the presence of higher and nobler claims, uses, and joys, no loss of real pleasure is ever called for by the demands of Christian love.

This law of love then is the law of the body's true development, use, welfare, and pleasure.

Intelligently obeyed, this central force of Christianity will make the most of man intellectually. The intellect, being one of the most important factors of manhood, Christian love demands that it be made the most and highest possible, and then used as an instrument for the advancement and elevation of man.

Christianity — however misconceived, and sometimes by its own friends — is no bat or mole, choosing " darkness rather than light." Believing that He who made facts made also the mind to know them, it seeks to find all truth, and use it for the good of man. And since no scheme or labor for the good of man can be permanently successful so long as it ignores any essential fact, it will seek to cover or blink no truth however disagreeable, or however destructive it may be to old and cherished theories.

But while it is not only right, but commendable to seek intellectual truth as an end in itself, in so far as such seeking interferes with no higher call; yet the search for facts is not in itself Christian, and may be positively and greatly evil. A selfish gratification of the passion for laws and theories and facts, may be as far one side of the pathway of a true love, as is the life of the basely sensual. Reading earth's geologic record, spying out the microscopic marvels of the globe, weighing the planets, tracing the roadways of the stars; and in the sphere of human relationships, developing the laws of political economy and the constitutions of states; any and all study may, under certain circumstances, be contrary to the law of love, and so unchristian and inhumane. Development of the brain alone may be either toward or away from that which is right. And so, of itself, and for itself, the principle of Christian love forbids it.

But since the brain is an engine of power, and so capable of great achievement in the direction of human welfare, love makes its highest culture and most unselfish use a duty. The Christian should do the most he can to make his brain as perfect and powerful a machine as possible for the discovery and application of truth. And then he must use it to stimulate, develop, lift up, and push forward the life of the world.

True Christianity then, so far from repressing investigation and shackling the intellect of man, for fear that, Samson-like, his untamed strength may rudely tear down the pillars of its antique structure, will only open shutters, pull off blinkers, and let in the light. For if God made and controls all things there is nothing to fear. And whatever of restriction or

fear there has been in the past, or may
be in the present, is no part of real Christianity. They are only the trembling of
superstitious or faithless souls who fear
the tumbling down of man-made and
weak-foundationed structures. The true
love of man, which is true Christianity,
requires that all possible truth be found
and used for the help of the world. And
whoever hinders this free search and use,
is false to the fundamental principle of
Christianity, as set forth in the Master's
own words.

And, in the third place, the principle
of Christianity will develop to the highest and best the affectional nature of
man. It equally forbids the repression
or perversion of the heart.

Such a thing as loving a person or a
thing too much is impossible. You cannot love a friend too much, nor home too
much, nor country too much, nor this
world too much. They are worthy of

all the affection you can lavish on them. And for his own development a man can no more love too much than the sun can shine too brightly, or a diamond be too brilliant. The glory and beauty are in the shining, and the brilliance, and the loving. And yet it is common to hear mothers told that God will take away a child for their loving it. And people are made to feel that they ought to hate God's good world.

But though these are mistakes, there may be fault in our loving, and true Christianity may condemn it. It is not loving too much, but too exclusively. The love ought to go out, not less toward the one object, but toward others more. If selfish affections control the life, they make it narrow, exclusive, proud, ungenerous, unmindful of the wider life and wants of the world. Let love flow freely, only subordinate the lower affections to the higher.

The heart also may be perverted to the love of things unworthy, false, and wrong. This also, since it stands in the way of personal growth toward the highest, and hinders the progress of the world, a true Christian love forbids.

Only let the force of Christianity have free play in the heart then, and it will call out all its powers, and direct them toward that which is noblest and best. It is thus seen to be the principle of perfection in the affectional nature.

And once more, it will work with equal success in the higher realm of the religious life.

If man be indeed an immortal spirit, and it be possible for him to enter into conscious relationship with the Father of spirits, then it becomes at once apparent that here is the widest, grandest, and most important field for human action. It bears on the permanent interests of humanity as nothing else can. It opens a sphere of duty that encompasses and subordinates every other.

That love then which regards the highest welfare of man seizes upon this as that which must be made the end and crown of all worldly aim and activity. It will give chief attention to this godward faculty as being in fact chief in rank and importance. And at the same time that it develops the spiritual nature to the highest, it forbids all its distortions and falsities. It condemns the excess of mystic meditation, as being selfish; for selfish enjoyment of God, or selfish soul-saving is no more Christian than selfish money-getting. It condemns the pride of spiritual insight; for any rejoicing in yourself as " elect," or " set apart," or " peculiarly favored," is unchristian. Paul's "I could wish myself accursed from Christ for my brethren," more truly gives it utterance. But since the maturity of immortality is more than the childhood of time, it places that first which is first, and makes the less give place to the more.

Put now the different parts together, and what is the composite individual that must result from the free working of the central force of Christianity? It is a perfect body, as the vehicle and servant of a perfect mind, both ruled and moulded by a love for the noblest and best, and all directed onward and upward in the hope of an immortality. Let him stand forth in imaged outline before you. Perfect body, perfect brain, perfect heart, all enshrining a spirit that looks godward; and the complete man started out on an immortal roadway that slopes endlessly upward, like the slanting glory of beams streaming downward from a rising sun. The body is good, and only gives way to that which is more important. And so the intellect is good, and only yields to that which outranks it. And the heart rules in its sphere, only bowing to the

5

supreme faculty of all. Thus the man is complete. No schism, no insubordination, no disorder. This is the perfect man.

Thus the unobstructed working of the force of Christian love will make the most and best possible of the individual; and then it will bring him, like true knight-errant of old, to devote himself unreservedly to the service of the highest welfare of the world. What nobler ideal of life ever has been, or can be conceived? And this is neither less nor more than that toward the attainment of which the central impulse of Christianity is bearing every one who puts himself in its current.

CHAPTER II.

COMPLETENESS in its parts implies the perfection of the whole. Thus, since the law of Christian love will produce perfection in the individual, so it must do nothing less for society. For if the life of each man and woman is right, the life of hundreds or thousands of them together must be right, and society is only aggregations of individuals. There can be no discord or wrong where all are working for the good of all. Only let this Christian love have full sway then, and the social life of the world were perfect. There is no jar, no wrong, no evil thought or wish, or word, or act, but is just a sin against this principle of love. Of families, cliques, churches, organizations, institutions, trade, commerce, and of all the ten thousand forms that our social relations assume, the same holds true. Not one namable evil can be found but the law of Christian love forbids and would destroy.

This principle also holds the secret of the highest and grandest political hope of the world, a true comity of nations. If ever a true statesmanship is to rule the world, if ever diplomacy is to be anything better than the attempt of one people to outwit another, if ever nations are to bend their concerted energies to the well-governing and elevation of men, all will be but the application of this one principle to international regulations. There can be nothing higher than the outflowing of this principle. If ever then the dream of prophet is to harden into fact; if what is true and noble in the longings of philosophy, as in Plato's "Republic," is to be realized; if John's "City of God" is ever to come down out of heaven; if Herbert

Spencer's " equilibrium" is to give equipoise to the unbalanced state of the
world; it must all be by the supremacy
and regnant force of Christian love. No
conception of human perfection ever has
been, or ever can be, that, though it
leave out the principle, does not include
as necessary a course of action precisely
such as this principle tends to produce.
So that the highest and best of what the
world dreams of and hopes for is only
what Christianity offers to give, and is
giving, so far as it is intelligently accepted and obeyed.

Now just stand off in imagination and
get the proportions of this grand cosmos
of humanity that ranges itself round this
central idea.

If you could stand outside the solar
system, and had such a range of vision as
would take it in, and include all in one
glance, so that it would look like one
vast fleet of worlds sailing through space

around, and ordered by, its great Sun-ad-
miral, — and if you could, at the same
time, see the microscopic wonders of each
planet and asteroid and moon, you might
have some idea of the all-inclusive sweep,
of the minute and magnificent power of
gravitation. You might see how each
atom of sand, tossed by the wind; how
each leaf swaying in the summer air; how
every ocean-current and mighty tide and
tiny curl and cap of white-fringed wave;
how the orbit of every moon, the whirl of
Saturn's rings, the sweep of each ponder-
ous planet, — how all is held in the grip,
and determined by the force of this wondrous gravitation, that overlooks nothing
infinitesimal, and holds a kingly sway
over all that is immense.

And such as gravitation is in the physical universe, making a cosmos of chaos,
such is the law of Christian love in the
world of humanity. Nothing escapes it,
nothing is too high for it, from the hidden

movement of thought or wish in the individual breast, to the grandest developments of society, or the movements of nations. Everywhere it comes as the principle of order. Having free and full sway, it would produce as perfect a cosmos of humanity as gravitation has already produced of the material world. Every step of progress that the world has ever taken, or can take, is but a step toward the realization of this idea.

CHAPTER III.

DEFECTS OF OTHER THEORIES — RELIGIOUS.

PERHAPS it will now be granted that the true manhood must be built on the principle of love as its corner-stone. For whatever progress towards its perfection humanity has already made, has been produced by the inspiration of love; or else, from prudential motives, such courses of conduct have been followed as the influence of love would have brought about. For instance, a true study of the laws of political economy reveals the fact that it is for the pecuniary and industrial interest of nations to maintain such mutual relations with each other as the law of Christian love demands. And now many are selfishly laboring for such relations. But this, and all similar facts, bear witness to the truth of Christianity. It may be taken for granted then that the law of Christian love holds the key to the world's perfection.

But the question will arise with many, as to whether this theory of manhood is original with Christianity, and can thus be made a basis on which to raise its claims. This attitude of question is that of thousands at the present time. Granting the truth of its main ideas, doesn't it share this truth with many others? A negative form of the Golden Rule is found in Confucius. Many or most of Christ's moral maxims can be culled, like scattered flowers, from ancient heathen sages, and so bound into as fair a bouquet as the Sermon on the Mount. Even the incomparable Lord's Prayer itself can be found, a thought here, a petition there, like pieces of a broken mosaic, among the Hebrew writings and traditions that preceded Christ. May not one be built up

on the Christian model then, and still not
be a Christian? Can Christianity claim
an absolute supremacy, as having for its
peculiar possession this gift of love that
holds the secret of the world's perfection?
May not a man follow the lead of some
other guide, and yet attain the perfect
manhood?

On the answer to such questioning
hangs a great deal. If others can also
teach the true manhood, then Christianity must be content to be one sister in
a family of religions; and Christ is but
one teacher among many. But if this
ideal of man be found nowhere but in
Christianity, then is it exalted to an un-
shared supremacy, and claims sole pre-
rogative in the human heart. The solution of the problem is a historical one.
It can be answered simply by looking at
facts. Will you stand by my side .then
while we ask the religions and systems
of the world to file by, and submit to our

brief inspection? Our review of each must be very short. But then we only wish to ask them each one question. We will look for the central principle of each claimant for the homage of humanity, and find out what kind of a man conformity to it would make. If it does not stand the test of the true manhood, then it must be voted defective, and pass by. If it does, then Christianity must give up its supremacy. Ask each one then what kind of a man it would make.

It is a fundamental principle of all science that a true theory must find room for and explain all important facts. If it cannot do this it is thereby proved untrue. For instance, the Ptolemaic theory of the universe was based on the assumption that the earth was the centre. So soon as it was found that the sun was central, the theory was abandoned. It did not account for facts, and so must fall. Any theory of humanity then that ignores or perverts the facts of the world, or of human nature, that does not find room for all the parts and capabilities of man, and that does not give him room to unfold the possibilities, that like leaves in a bud are wrapped within him,—any such theory is defective, and therefore false. Try the other systems by this test.

1. Confucianism. Confucius was born B. C. 551, making him contemporary with the return of the Jews from the Babylonish Captivity, and of the invasion of Greece by Xerxes. No man who ever lived, except the writers of the Bible, has exerted by his writings so wide-spread and so enduring an influence on the world as he. He is to-day the classical model of the most populous nation on the globe. He published an admirable system of practical morals. Many of his maxims are as wise as those of Solomon. Long before the time of Christ he gave his people a negative form of the Golden Rule.

But the central idea of the system is *reverence for the past, and a prudential morality, working on humanity from without, through a system of rules, and having for its end the fixed stability of the social and governmental order.* Its natural result is mental, moral, social, artistic, and political stagnation. It is the apotheosis of conservatism. It finds all wisdom in the graves of the past. It teaches no certain immortality, and inspires with no thought of progress. It looks upon all change as the precursor of anarchy, — the loss of present good, and not the addition of more. Its result is order; but it is the order of a crystal, or of death, not of a living growth. Instead of the orderly flow and growth of a river that broadens and deepens ever onward, it is a painted river, that is forever the same. It is the stability of arctic frost and ice.

It gives man no adequate future, hope, or room for advance. It only tells him to be prudent, and keep what he has. It fails to conceive man's true greatness, and has for him no worthy destiny. Instead of being a leading genius to go on before humanity, it comes and looks into its face with the awful, fixed gaze of Medusa, and turns it into a statue, to stand forever with stony eyes staring backward.

2. Brahmanism, the dominant religion of India, is one of the oldest of the world. We can trace it back two or three thousand years, but cannot find its source. It makes so little of this world and its transactions that it has counted it of small importance to make or keep historic records.

Its essential idea is, that *there is no true, real existence but spirit. This world, finite souls, time, space, matter, all are illusions.* All forms of life and activity are only manifestations of the one, all pervasive, pantheistic Brahm; just as the waves are all parts of the great one ocean.

Gods, and men, and animals, and trees, and worlds, rise out of and fall back into this great unity of spirit, the only real thing that lives. And this Brahm himself is not consciously existent, except as he wakes up into the various forms of transitory, personal being ; but is eternally absorbed in a sort of day-dream of slumberous self-contemplation. There isn't any good, and there isn't any evil ; all are shadow and illusion alike. There is nothing but shadow. As strange, and incomprehensible as it may seem to us, the only *real evil* to the Brahman is *conscious, individual existence.* By some inexplicable fate, he has become entangled in a series and succession of births and deaths. That is, each one has already lived many lives in other bodies, of man, or fish, or bird, or animal, before being born into the present one. And he is liable to live many more. To be thus so many times born, to be subject to the ups and downs, and changes of existence, — this is the great evil. And salvation, the one great and desirable thing, is to escape the tedious round of births, and become absorbed forever in the quiescence of Brahm. When this is attained, the good Hindoo will never think, nor feel, nor suffer, nor change again. He will sleep forever, as a part of the one great all.

The way to attain this salvation is through a contemplative life, and the utter mortification and destruction of the flesh. Hence the swinging on flesh-hooks, hanging by the feet over fires, lying on beds of thorns, sticking the body full of pins, holding up arms till they grow stiff and fleshless. Life being an evil, all virtue consists in crushing it out.

It hardly needs that the defects of this system be pointed out. It not so much fails to account for the facts of humanity as it ignores them. The world is nothing, and life an evil, and reabsorption in the infinite the only real good. And this good is consciously nothing at all.

3. Buddhism, the system which has more followers than any other on the globe, dates its origin some seven hundred years before the birth of Christ. Its founder, Sakya-Muni, was a prince of one of the Northern nations of India. It branches off from Brahmanism somewhat as Christianity does from Judaism. Its forms of worship and organization strikingly resemble Catholicism. Like Brahmanism, it counts the great evil of life to be its ceaseless rounds and changes. Its chief aim is to reach Nirvâna, which means either non-existence, or, more probably, a life free from care and change, far above all the fluctuations of this lower life. The way to Nirvâna is through obedience to the laws of nature and a practical virtue. But, as it conceives man capable of this himself, and as needing no outside help, it ignores God and is

practically atheistic. Yet, since humanity will have some object of worship, his followers have deified their founder, and the Buddha has become their God. Its central idea is, *the selfish salvation of the individual soul from the rounds and changes of continued earthly existence, by contemplation of truth and good works.*

Its defects are many. It ignores God. It gives little or no hope of a personal, conscious future. Instead of holding up an infinite beauty and good to draw the soul out of itself into a large and divine life, it simply surrounds a man with law, and tells him to keep it, or suffer. There is no hope, no inspiration; God is nothing, the future is nothing, and the present is hard and sad. Buddhism sees hell, but not divine love nor heaven. Existence is a hopeless evil, and the greatest of all good is never to have been born at all. Such a system cannot make manhood, nor society, nor government. It is the religion of despair.

4. The time when Zoroaster lived is involved in great obscurity. It is known that he was at least as ancient as Moses or Abraham. And some good authorities make him to have lived five or six thousand years before Christ.

He divides the universe between two gods, Ormazd, the god of light, and Ahriman, the god of darkness. The one creates all the good in the universe, the other all the evil; and they are in eternal war with each other.

The central thought of Zoroastrianism is this *eternal battle between light and darkness, good and evil.* Its great error is in thus making a dualism of gods, and marking as essentially evil a thousand things which are only good in the making, or else are evil only because of perversion or excess. Instead of completing manhood by development and symmetrical arrangement of all its parts, it blights and exterminates some of the essentials of his

being. Its great propelling motives are
duty and fear. It is right in its thought
of a great warfare with darkness and sin.
It is wrong in making the evil principle
equal to the good. And it fails in not
appealing to the great principle of love
in humanity, and so binding all together
in the glad and willing service of the one
supreme, the Father in heaven.

5. The religions of Greece and Rome
are linked together in the fact that their
conceptions of the gods, and of spiritual
life were similar. The deities that peopled Olympus were the different phases,
powers, and passions of humanity person-
ified and deified. The supreme conception of Greece was beauty ; and it natu-
rally flowered out into the highest art
that the world has ever seen. Idolizing
beauty as they did, and this beauty being
chiefly physical and intellectual, the Grecian type of manhood runs all to sense or
intellect. Of morality it made little, of

the spirit nothing. The gods had little relation with human life, and the future held out no hope that was inspiring, even if accepted; while many believed in none at all. Thus the Grecian theory of manhood leaves out the most important factors, and offers no adequate career.

The Romans made law and the supremacy of the state its great idea. Its supernaturalism was substantially the same as the Grecian; but its ideal of human life was different. It was a hard system of external rules. These rules ended in an oppressiveness that stifled life; and the result was a dying out of morals in the utter decay and dissolution of the later empire.

Build a man on the Roman model, and he becomes the stern, law-abiding citizen. But the system has all the hardness of the Mosaic ritual, — something that no one is " able to bear." The elements of hope, and love, and a helping God are utterly lacking.

6. Mohammed was born in the latter part of the sixth century. Within a hundred years from the Hegira (A. D. 622) the faith of Islam had conquered all Arabia, Syria, Persia, Northern Africa, and Spain. At one time it seriously threatened to overrun Europe. Its creed is *a bald monotheism, absolute and unchanging decrees, the divine mission of Mohammed to exterminate all infidels, a hell of literal fire, and a heaven of sensuous indulgences and delights after a final resurrection of the flesh.*

The ideal man of Islam is he who can cry " Allah is Allah, and Mohammed is his prophet," and who, for this creed, is ready to sacrifice relatives, friends, country, even life itself. He may be ignorant, treacherous, cruel, sensual, anything, so far as character is concerned, and yet look forward to the highest reward of the faithful

It is even his duty to " do evil that good may come." Any and every true and noble element of manhood may be left out, and yet, if faithful to his creed and system, the beautiful houris await him in his paradise above.

CHAPTER IV.

DEFECTS OF OTHER THEORIES — SCIENTIFIC AND PHILOSOPHIC.

SUBJECT now to the same brief test the principal scientific and philosophic substitutes for Christianity.

1. Modern Pantheism. This acknowledges as its father, Benedict Spinoza, a German Jew, born at Amsterdam, A. D. 1632. Spinoza himself was a man of irreproachable life and morals. He believed in a state religion as part of a proper governmental order: but denied the right of the state to interfere with anything save the externals. Belief and feeling were to be left free.

The system of pantheism teaches that *all existence is but a manifestation of the one, or the all, which lies back of it.*

Stars, planets, trees, waters, animals, and man are, all and each, but differing manifestations of this one that comprehends the whole. They emerge from, and sink back into, the one.

And since God is everything and everything is God, there is no such thing as individual freedom. We are but links of a chain, drawn along by the one ahead of us, and drawing after us another.

And as freedom is an essential part of any right or wrong, in denying freedom, pantheism denies any virtue or vice. It allows no moral distinction between them any more than between light and darkness, or between an agreeable and an offensive odor. It allows the right of human government to punish and reward for its own protection, and to secure social order. But it punishes a criminal, not with any moral indignation, but for the same reason that one would kill a snake in his yard, or fill up a bog-hole in his neighborhood, for fear of malaria and disease.

It believes in the world's growing better and higher : but nobody has anything in particular to do about it, more than grass has about growing.

As its prominent defects I mark these. It has no personal God, and offers no personal existence in the future. These take out of it the elements of future hope. It has nothing to live for beyond this life, and no freedom of choice as to what even it shall be. It does not claim to make a true man, nor a perfect race. It does indeed point to a developed world somewhere down the ages ; but the individuals now living bear about the same relation to it that last year's leaves bear to the bloom and fruitage of the coming season. Instead of *perfecting* individual humanity it *extinguishes* it.

2. Another system that proposes to take the place of Christianity is Positivism. It originated with M. Auguste Compte, a French philosopher, born A. D.

1798. Glance at its principles, and see what it can do for humanity.

Its first position is, that the human mind, in its progress, passes through three stages. The *first* of these is the Theological, wherein it refers all things to divine causes and agents. The *second* is the Metaphysical, in which it deals with the abstractions of the mind. And the *third* and last stage is that of the Positive Philosophy. When arrived here, men give up trying to know anything beyond observed material facts and changes. Out of its positive sciences, it builds up a hierarchy, in which Sociology ranks supreme; and here for a time it stopped. But finding that men would have some kind of a religion, it proposed what it called the *religion of humanity.* It taught that since man could know nothing higher than himself, therefore his grandest ideal could be nothing higher than that of universal humanity, figured forth as the *Grand Be-*

ing. And this sum total of humanity it offered to itself as its god. As illustrations of this high humanity, it encouraged special homage toward the great and illustrious of the past.

It utterly ignores the supernatural. It has no word to say of God, of the soul, or of any future hope. Man can only look at the facts about him and die; and that is all. It offers no adequate sup port for human virtue, and no adequate scope for human progress. It has only a body and an intellect, and a heart for the earth-side of life. The upward affections, and the spirit, it leaves wholly out of its account.

3. And now a word in general about Modern Science, as represented by Darwin, Spencer, Huxley, and Tyndall.

It is neither brave nor wise to share in the theologic fears of these men and their teachings. What is true will remain; what is false will crumble away. And

it is hard to see what there is about
their well-substantiated teachings that the
Christian need fear to accept.

But when they go so far as to touch the
essentials of religion, and offer their systems in the place of Christianity, they have
simply stepped over the lines that mark
off their proper field, and are meddling
with those things to which their scientific
methods are not adequate. In their field
they are supreme. They have a right
to correct the erroneous speculations of
Christianity in the realm of physics. But
because they cannot find the soul with
the dissecting scalpel, or discover the bat-
tlements of heaven with a telescope, or
find the spiritual God in the chemist's
crucible, they have hardly the right to
assume that they do not exist. Human
intuition of God and spiritual things is as
authoritative in its sphere as their experiments are in theirs.

And beside, they are even unscientific

in their scientific assaults on religion. A true science of religion must recognize and make room for all essential facts. Now the religious instinct, the demand for God, the impulse to prayer, the longing for immortality — these all are *facts*, facts just as substantial as bodies, and bones, and rocks, and gases; and they are facts absolutely universal.

Since this is so, nothing can be more unscientific than to ignore them. They must be taken into account, recognized as parts of humanity, and have their place and function assigned them by any system that undertakes to be the science of humanity.

But physical science professes to be able to deal with only the tangible, ponderable facts of the world. Therefore it can never take the place of religion, nor leave religion behind.

And now, after this rapid survey, let us turn back to Christianity. All these

other systems have much that is good
about them. They were not originated
by the devil for the misleading of humanity. They are the attempts of mankind after truth and good. So far as
they are true, they came from and were
inspired by God. Confucianism, in its
morality, and clinging to the good of the
past; Brahmanism, in its firm grasp of
spiritual reality; Buddhism, in its search
for virtue; Zoroastrianism, in its eternal
hostility to darkness; Greece and Rome,
in their deification of beauty and law;
Mohammedanism, in its supreme loyalty
to the one God; Pantheism, in its recognition of the real presence and working of
God everywhere; Positivism, in its exaltation of the ideal of humanity; and
Modern Science, in its strong grip of the
facts of the universe; these all are right
and true and god-like. But each one has
essential evils, and lacks essential goods.
All are partial; and neither of them

gives a model after which the true manhood can be built. They all leave out some important factor of the individual; and none has any adequate hope for the race. You cannot, from the principles of either of them, construct a complete individual, society, or nation.

But Christianity assumes and holds an absolute supremacy over them all; and this supremacy it bases on the fact that it includes them all, and more. There is not a single good, or truth, or beauty in any of them that is not a natural part of Christianity; and at the same time it supplies the deficiencies of them all. It includes them all in its own higher development, just as man includes in himself all the forms of life beneath him. It has room in it for all the facts of the world, and all the facts of human nature. It gives scope, and offers free play to, and makes room for the development of every capacity and possibility of manhood. Its field is eternity: its scope and end the God and Father and Maker of all: its life an endless progress and unfolding: its hope and promise the completion of all that is best in the individual, and the unity of all in the grand family of man. It lacks nothing, it gives all. Man cannot ask for good which it cannot bestow; nor can he conceive of its ever being outgrown.

Christianity then must stand. A crowned creature of eternity, it contains nothing in its essential life that can decay. It has the step of immortal vigor. On its thigh is the sword of universal conquest and dominion; and in its eyes, that look before and after, the light of divinity, and the tender look of helpfulness and love.

CHAPTER V.

THE religions and philosophies of the world, outside of Christianity, offer theories for the acceptance of man. They embody these theories in institutions, through which they seek to realize them in the life of humanity. But no one of them appeals to any universal attribute of humanity, or claims to make itself a power of life in those who accept it. And yet just these two things must any religion do that professes with any show of reason to be adequate to its work.

The problem is to make humanity what it ought to be, — to take it just where it is, and build it up after its ideal pattern. The religion then that undertakes this work must be capable of appealing to every human being, in whatever condition or stage of development; and at the same time of becoming in him an adequate power of help, so that he may be able to do what he thinks and dreams and wishes. Of what value would the sun's warmth be to the plants, if it could only come to the young sprouts, and say, " Grow till you're six inches tall, and then I'll help you?" or, if it should say, "I'll help the roses and the dahlias, but such common stuff as grass and cabbages must look out for themselves?" Sunshine that doesn't touch and vitalize every living thing is no sunshine at all, any more than Shakespeare's clown, with his lantern and thorn-bush, is the moon. He may personate and play moon forever; but that which makes moonlight is the possession of the qualities of moonlight. And so this, or that, or another system may claim to be the true religion. But the decisive question is, Has it the qualities, and can it do the work of the true religion?

We have seen that the true religion must be able to come to every man, and then become in him a power of living it out. None but Christianity meets these conditions. They all fail in one or the other or both of these. Some of them appeal to ambition; some to pride; some to sensuality; some to despair of the world; some to fear. Some of them combine two or more of these in various kinds and degrees of mixture. But no one of these is central and universal in man. A religion that is chiefly intellectual can reach only the intellectual; one of fear only the superstitious and craven; and so on through them all. They all must be partial, because they build on what only a part of humanity possesses, or is governed by.

But love is the one absolutely universal attribute of humanity. And not only is it in every man, it is central and dominant in every man. It rules him. Whatever then can command the love can command the man.

It is found also that this universal human love can most readily be called out towards persons. Principles are too abstract for the lowest grades of human development. But the capability of loving a person is what no human being has ever yet been found to lack. If then a religion can be found combining all that humanity needs, — principles, sentiments, enthusiasms, truths, — in the love of a person, it will answer the highest, and every condition that we can conceive of as necessary to a universal religion. The love that follows a guide, though it may lack wisdom and power, does yet have all it wants in the love that links it to him who posesses all. A little child may be utterly incapable of navigating a ship from New York to San Francisco. Yet, loving, trusting and sailing with his father, who is a navigator, gives him as safe a voyage as though he knew and did it all. The timbers of the hulk, the sails, the rudder, the compass, the quadrant, the winds, and the stars, all become servants to his trusting love.

Just herein is the peculiarity of Christianity, and here is its fitness for universality. Any being who can love has access to all the needed knowledge of God. The Christ, as the manifestation of God to the world, offers to the love of man, in his own person, all that is fairest, noblest, highest, best. And he who loves and follows Him progressively lives all best things, though he know but few. Though he be no theologian, he lives the highest theology. Though philanthropy as a system be unknown, he lives the truest philanthropy. Though political economy be all unread, he lives the highest political economy. Though no socialistic philosopher, he lives for the best interests of society. And so all truth, and all good, he advances to-

ward, and lives out, unknowing. Whatever the wisdom of the highest can do
for them, love for Him who is the highest wisdom can do for him.

Love then being the central, govern-
ing principle of humanity, the one that is
universal, possessed by all nations, classes,
grades, and men, the religion that is true
must make its appeal to this. Just this
is what Christianity, and no other religion, does. It is therefore capable of universality. And since it, and it alone, is thus
capable, it herein bears the unimpeach-
able credential of truth.

But further than this, we have seen
that it also makes claim to the other essential attribute of the absolute religion, that
is, that it should be able to take humanity
where it is, and become in it a vital force
of growth toward the fulfillment of its perfect manhood. This it does by presenting
to the human heart a perfect and attractive
personal ideal, — an ideal that can draw

the lowest in morality, and least cultured in intellect, while at the same time, it is no less attractive and stimulating to the highest and best. Here then, in presenting the person of the Christ as the manifestation of God to the love of man, is the distinguishing feature of Christianity. And this presentation answers the demand of the highest conception of religion that we can form. It becomes in men a power of loving and following the highest. As an illustration of what is meant by the power of the Christ as contrasted with that of any other, take the words of Napoleon : " Alexander, Cæsar, Charlemagne, and myself have founded empires. But upon what did we rest the creations of our genius ? Upon force. Jesus Christ alone founded his empire upon love ; and at this moment millions of men would die for Him. I die before my time, and my body will be given back to earth to become food for worms. Such is the fate of him who has

been called the Great Napoleon. What
an abyss between my deep misery, and
the eternal kingdom of Christ, which is
proclaimed, loved, and adored, and which
is extended over the whole earth! Call
you this dying? Is it not living rather?"

CHAPTER VI.

CHRISTIANITY A POWER OF SELF-REALIZATION.

How the person of the Christ is a power it is now our business to trace out; and,

1. It is a power of arresting the attention and holding the interest of the world. Jesus said, "And I, if I be lifted up, will draw all men unto me." And this attracting power of his person is one of the most wondrous things in Christianity. Did you ever meditate upon it so as to take in its significance?

And it holds, without answering, the curiosity of all men and all times alike. Confucius, Socrates, Mohammed, — these men have no such personal hold on humanity. We follow their careers, read their maxims, and put them one side as beings comprehensible like ourselves. We do not feel that what they were, or did, or said is of any great importance, or practical concern to us. Their interest is a purely historical one. But the Christ comes ever freshly before us, an unreadable sphinx for our curiosity, and a perpetual challenge to our moral sense. We cannot put Him one side. His person haunts us with the suggestion that it is of infinite importance for us to know his claims upon us, and the basis on which they are founded.

And you must not think it a small matter that it is made the Christ's first power over humanity that He appeals to its curiosity. Unless Christianity began here, it would lack one main proof of being divine. If we could classify and arrange it, and put it away on the shelf, we should be done with it. What makes the difference, in the interest we feel toward them, between a common pond and the ocean? We can walk around a pond, and fathom it, and know it all in an hour. The ocean is a perpetual mystery. We walk along its margin, and it casts up ever some new gift at our feet. We sail on its bosom, or dredge its deeps, and compel it ever to some new utterance of its infinity. We sit on its rocks in childhood, and then again when our years are upon us, or in old age, and the same mystic song, tumultuous in its thunders on the cliffs, or mellow in tiny ripples on the sand, holds us by its fascinating spell. Like Scheherezade, it has always a story that we wish to hear, and is never done.

In this, Christianity is at one with all that God has made. Childhood and flowers never tell us their mystery; and so we never tire of them. You can no more explain a violet than you can the universe. And the insoluble marvel of life ever looks up anew from the new-born baby's eyes. Astronomy is a perpetual attraction, because it holds in its recesses new glories to be revealed. The "Northwest Passage" has an irresistible attraction, because of secrets not yet unfolded. A thousand men will be interested to pick a lock where not a hundred care what is in the room beyond. This insatiable curiosity is an attribute, and one of the most important attributes of humanity. Thus the religion of humanity must grasp and hold this faculty by something ever beyond it.

Herbert Spencer defines knowledge as simply a process of classification. For instance, I see a new flower, and I say, "That is a kind of rose." I know the flower after that. Or I find a new animal, and I say, "He is of the canine species." I know him then. And, as he says, that which cannot thus be classified cannot be intellectually known. Thus it follows inevitably, that if Christianity is above and beyond all other religions, it must be forever a mystery. If it could be classified with other religions, it would thereby appear to be no more than they. Because it is divine and true, it must forever be an unanswered challenge to the human mind.

Thus, like the ocean, like mountains, like childhood, like the starry heavens, like the life and mind of man, Christianity, having upon it the finger marks of God's infinity, is fitted to attract and hold the attention of the world throughout all time. It can never be solved, tied up in a paper, and laid away on the shelf of humanity's past.

2. It is a perpetual condemnation of human imperfection. As a model, as an ideal, as a presence, as a guardian, as a companion, this is true.

All sense of imperfection and wrong comes by comparison and contrast. And whatever else Christianity may or may not have done, it has hung in the heaven of man's eternal consciousness an unapproachable moral ideal. So glorious is its excellence, and so all-searching is its power, that no one can escape it except as the sunshine may be avoided, — by hiding away from it in the dark. "It is the light that enlightens every man coming into the world." So that Jesus may justly say, "If I had not come and spoken unto them they had not had sin; but now they have no cloak for their sin."

The Christ is a model by which to measure our endeavor, and by which in fact all the morality of the world is consciously or unconsciously tried. As the young sculptor works with mallet and chisel, turning again and again, hour after hour, to his model, to correct his thought and guide his blows, so do men turn to the Christ. Whether or not the world confesses his claim to originate and bestow, it does regard Him as embodying and representing the moral character of the race.

He is in the mind and heart an ever-growing and expanding ideal of moral beauty. He forever stands above where we are to condemn our not being further.

Just as a painter's ideal grows with his mental development and artistic attainment, keeping always ahead of him. Perfect beauty and execution are so much larger than his thought that he can never outgrow them. Thus ranks the central person of Christianity. An ideal of moral beauty that can never be completely thought, He forever condemns contentment with partial attainment.

As a felt presence of purity and nobility He works ever a convincer of sin. He haunts the mind of those who have been trained under the influence of his teaching and character, as a loving and reproving presence. Other great characters of history share this power according to their greatness and the truth which they embodied. Alexander lived under the forming influence of Homer in his Achilles. Plato walked in the shadow of Socrates. And so all the master minds of the world have exerted a singular beneficent or blighting power over the minds of those who have lived under their shadow. But the Christ is the supreme example of such a force, because He is the supreme mind and heart of the world. We cannot shake ourselves free from his presence. If we will not walk in the light, but choose cellars and caves instead, even there a stray beam through an unexpected chink, or the bright memory of the upper radiance, will still come to tell us how dark and cheerless we are.

As a guardian also He convinces. No man who had seen it, was ever yet able to forget his mother's face. And though grown to never so independent a manhood, could he feel himself set free from allegiance to the moral queenliness of the gently - commanding countenance. And this, not because mother's eyes had anything like a sword behind them. They demand obedience by the simple force of the moral truth and love that look through them. They rule, because they are above us, on a height we ought to occupy, and because they bid us come up higher. All the omnipotence of God's eternal right is in their mildness. And so, the Christ. Embodying the righteousness of God, He becomes of necessity an authoritative guardian of our life. And when He beckons us away from evil towards Himself, it is with all the authority of God's everlasting and unchanging truth and right and beauty.

And as an inseparable companion He reproves and convicts. I have looked into faces that made me blanch; and they were always the faces of those whom I looked up to as better than I. They searched me, as if one walked through the chambers of my soul with a candle, peering into every unswept corner, seeing every foul picture, uncovering every hidden possession. I have always had almost a superstitious awe in looking upon the portrait of one of my dead brothers; and yet no brother was ever loved more than he. The love and awe blend, and are one. He always seemed to me wondrously pure and noble. And now as I sit and write, I look up at his face, or as I walk my study and stand before his picture, I feel so deeply his loving companionship in my inmost soul, that I become ashamed of everything I ever thought or did, that I feel he would have disapproved. As such a loving brother does the person of the Christ come to every soul of man. As such He is felt by all those who receive him. With loving reproof and winning counsel, his unspotted companionship condemns our sins, and turns shame and self-reproach into motives for better living.

Thus as a power of moral conviction the Christ stands perfect. Nothing higher for this part of the work of the absolute religion can possibly be conceived.

3. This person of the Christ, the central force of Christianity, has also an infinite power for creating a new life in man.

This power of the Christ is like the power of the sun in spring. Simply by hanging over the earth and shining does the sun drive away winter, and bring in the beauty and glory of June. The very bluster of March storms and the gusts of March winds, are but results of the rousing and quickening power that will destroy them. The season may halt, or even seem to turn back upon its course, but the presence of the sun on high makes us certain that the frost king's reign is broken, and the scent of spring buds will soon be on all the air. Thus " the glory of God in the face of Jesus Christ" shines ever down upon the world of men. And beneath its power icy indifference melts, clouds of doubt dissipate, new life springs out of the death and decay of the past, and the verdure and fragrance of a garden takes the place of the former desert.

No other system ever offered the power of a personal love as the regenerator of character. Drawn by the glory of their achievements, the splendor of their renown, or the attractions and excitements of army life, — some few, perhaps, by personal admiration, — men followed Alexander into Asia, or Napoleon over the Alps. But the Christ is the first great leader of history, who, by the power of his personal love, has drawn thousands of men out of, and away from their most fascinating passions, and their dearest sins. Not only embodying the severest outline of moral purity, He has clothed it with a fascination that makes the world go after it. He has discovered the secret of the human heart, and so drawn it into magnetic sympathy with his own, that in all its variations and vibrations, it is ever settling nearer and nearer to his true north.

It is said that every structure, as built, is pitched to some one musical key, so that he who can discover and sound its chord may control it at his will. The Christ has the key-note of humanity, and at the touch of his divine music, He makes it thrill and vibrate as He pleases. To quote Napoleon again: " Christ speaks, and at once generations become his by stricter, closer ties than those of blood, — by the most sacred, the most indissoluble of all ties. He lights up the flame of love which consumes self-love, which prevails over every other love. So that Christ's greatest miracle undoubtedly is the reign of charity."

There is no sin nor wrong in human nature, or in human life, but the love of the Christ has shown its power to uproot subdue, and overthrow. And this, not by force, which is unequal to it ; nor by fear, to which some are not susceptible ; nor by exhortations to prudence, which many will disregard; nor by abstract ideas of virtue, which only a few appreciate; but by the controlling and elevating power of a new love, capable of coming to all, which swallows up all lesser attractions as the sun puts out the stars.

And it would uproot all sin from all hearts, if only it could gain universal admittance. But the will holds the door. And if it should attempt to work by mechanical force, it would thereby disprove its claims. Mohammed may force his creed into men's hearts on the point of his scimitar, and they be neither better nor worse. Ritualism may herd men within its walls, and teach them to pronounce its shibboleths, and they be neither better nor worse. For since all moral action must be freely chosen action, mechanical force has no relation to human character. The Christ might smite with thunderbolts, or awe by miracles; but not thus would He be saving men from sin. Such being the nature of humanity and human action, the religion of humanity must be one of moral causes and moral results. And now,

4. The personal love of the Christ is an endless power of progress in the individual and in the race.

This claim is not made for many of the institutions that have grown up around, nor the accretions that cling to Christianity as a system. It can itself advance only by sloughing many of these. It is the personal love of the Christ that is the power of endless progression. His unapproachable ideal leads, and must forever lead the world. The disciples looked up to him, and said " Master," justifying the claim He made when He said, " You call me Master and Lord, and you say well; for so I am." And every century since has still looked up and said, " Master and Lord." For the high-water mark that humanity has touched in any extraordi-

nary individual has been indicated only
by comparison with Him. This one, we
say, exhibited some of the gentleness and
meekness of the Christ: that one, some of
his wondrous purity; another, something
of his divine charity; a fourth, a little of
his broad, world-wide superiority to national and sectional divisions. But no
one has dared to claim equality with Him
in any; much more, the completion of all
combined.

The absurdity of the thought of out-
stripping, or leaving behind the moral
ideal of the Christ, is too absurd for ref-
utation. As well might a ship-master
think to outsail and leave behind his horizon. Old landmarks may recede and
disappear, familiar constellations may
sink down the sky, new continents, new
climes, and strange civilizations may rise
to view, but the horizon ever advances,
encircles, and holds them all. So may
humanity sail down the ocean of the fu-

ture. Old headlands may sink, familiar forms go down in the receding distance, new and strange civilizations and forms of life and activity may arise, grow, sink behind, and in turn also disappear, and again give place to new. But the Christ ideal will still be wide as the sky, and grand as the cope of heaven. Unapproachable in the blue and spotless deeps of its infinity, it shall be the endless ocean for man to sail on, the boundless atmosphere for him to breathe, and the limitless space to shut him in, and give him infinite room.

And yet, so wondrous is the effect of this ideal, that, instead of crushing us by the sense of its being forever unattainable, it only stimulates and thrills with the sure hope of an endless advance. And this again is a divine adaptation. Man is such a being that the attainment of all that was possible to him, and a consequent stagnation, would be misery. If then he is to be immortal, there must be room for immortal advance. And this is found only in an unfathomable, unattainable ideal. So it is fitting, that while the Christ touches us on the side of our humanity, his life should still stretch off into the infinite, and manifest Him who is the All. If Christianity did not do this, it could not be true.

And now what have we gained by this chapter? We have found that Christianity, unlike any other system or religion, appeals to that in man which is universal, and comes as the power of a new life to all who will receive it. It not only brings theory, it turns it into fact. It not only offers an ideal, it makes that ideal a life. It not only tells men what to do and be, it helps them do and be it. It not only comes to the sick man, and tells him what health means, it makes him well. It not only outlines the true manhood, it progressively creates it.

PART III.

THE LESSON.

—◆—

CHAPTER I.

THE SPIRIT OF THE TIME.

If we seek a name for it, I know none better for the present period of the world's history than The Age of Criticism. Everybody is asking questions about everything. That which centuries have taken for granted is being examined anew. Men are asking it what foundation it stands on, and by what right it continues to exist. The earth and the heavens, governments, society, the Church, the individual, the ultimate principles of right and wrong, the very existence of the soul, and of a personal God, — these are being scrutinized as never before. Sys-

tems long supposed divine are proved
mortal, and overthrown. Theories long
unquestioned are found false, and cast
to the winds. What was considered au-
thentic history is turned into myth, and
blown away. It is a crucible time when
what is not gold has need to fear. Veneration for the old and established is
giving way to veneration for the true;
and what can be truer reverence? For
truth is ancient as God; and error, however old with men, is only a parvenu in
the reign of heaven.

The age then is not justly charged with
being irreverent. Never, since the world
began, was the heart of man so set on the
discovery of truth. "The truth, though
the heavens fall," might be taken as the
motto of the time. There is indeed a
rough grasping and shaking of time-hon-
ored institutions and usages; but it is
only to find out whether they have a
basis strong enough to uphold them, and

by which only they can prove their right to stand.

This searching and reconstruction is marked as the appointed mission of the age, by the fact that never before have there been such ample facilities for the work. So much has been brought to light in a generation, that it can hardly be called presumption to bring up for a new trial that which the wisest and best regarded as securely settled twenty-five years ago. Researches in geology and human antiquities, the comparative study of languages, mythologies, and religions, — these among others, have opened anew the old inquiries, have thrown a flood of light into dark places, and made it necessary to recast the old forms of thinking and doctrine.

And of all men in the world, the last to tremble at or oppose these movements should be the Christian. It is not faith in God, but a lack of it, that smothers inves-

tigation, that calls hard names, or offers
frantic and bigoted opposition. Whatever
is of God has in it God's eternity. That
which is simply of man may come to
nought, but what is of God no power can
overthrow.

> " Truth crushed to earth will rise again;
> The eternal years of God are hers."

The disciples of the truth then should not
fear to give her a free field and a naked
sword, and trust themselves to the issue.
It is the corporation that is unwilling to
have its books looked into that we are
ready to suspect. If a man places his
back against a door, and says it shall not
be opened, it begins to look as if it were
for his interest to keep it shut. He is a
poor friend to Christianity who sanctimo-
niously offers its sacredness as a reason
why it should not be looked at. It is
time we were through with such defense.
The world has had enough of it. If it is
true, it will bear scrutiny. If not, in

God's name, let us have done with it. Gold can bear tests. Only the dealers in brass need tremble.

One thing at least, in the midst of the general confusion, is clear; and that is, that whatever continues to exist, has got to give a reason for being. It must show cause why sentence of death should not be passed upon it. And this reason must be one of present force. It is not enough that a thing was good and satisfactory a hundred or a thousand years ago. It must hold in its hands cornucopias of present blessing and utility. It is not enough that it can offer strong proofs that it once came from the hands of God. It must have a present and living connection with the heavens. It would not warm and light the world to prove that a sun rose and shone, and became a source of growth and beauty a thousand years ago. We need a sun that rises and shines every day in the year.

And if we have this living presence and light we can put up with a flaw in the records of past shining, or even dispense with them altogether. But no continuity of records will enable us to dispense with the light and warmth. If Christianity then is to continue to rule the world, it must give some reason beyond the traditionally divine right of a long-descended sceptre. It must prove its right by its ability to adapt itself to the world's highest needs.

9

CHAPTER II.

BUT what is the condition of the ordinary " Evidences of Christianity " ? It is at least not too much to say, that they are inadequate.

Let us proceed to justify this statement. What have we of books and facts on which we can build? And how will our building stand the mining of adverse criticism ? It will not do to make out a list of what we suppose we need, and must have, and then incontinently declare that we have them. The method has been too often followed. So true is this, that the theological vision is proverbially regarded as warped, and gifted with seeing whatever is needful to make out its case. Let us then, for argument's sake, admit all that any one can have the face to demand.

So, for our present purpose, we will take the stand-point of the severe, outside critic, and see what he will allow us on our various claims. We will do this, because it is the opposer that we need to convince. It is time wasted to build up arguments that are useless except to those who already believe.

1. First then we have the books which are commonly bound together, and called the Bible.

As we offer these in proof of Christianity, our outside critic will tell us as follows : " In the first place, the canon of your Bible is not now, and never has been, definitely settled. Now this book, and now that, has been accepted, and set aside. The Council of Trent received as canonical all the apocryphal books of the Old Testament, and anathematized all who should reject them. They have been unanimously rejected by the Protestant world. And it is hard to give any but the book-binder's reason why the Book of Wisdom should not hold as high a place as Solomon's Song. And of the books still bound together by Protestants, the best scholarship of the world is still unsettled regarding Hebrews, James, Jude, 2d Peter, 2d and 3d John, and the Apocalypse.

"Then these books were written by many different writers, in many different nations, and the dates of their composition cover a long period of time. Of some of them it is true that nobody knows when, where, or by whom they were composed. Of many others the authorship, though not so .obscure, is still in dispute. And this, not only concerning those that are of little doctrinal consequence, and which are of equal value, no matter who wrote them ; but of the very central books of the New Testament.

Whether John was really the author of the Gospel that bears his name ; if he was, who wrote the Apocalypse ; or, if it is possible to reconcile the differences between them with the theory of identical authorship ; — these are questions that the foremost scholars and Christians of the age are in conflict over.

"Again, granting the authenticity and canonicity of them all, how do you know they have been handed down correctly ? We have only comparatively modern copies of books from two to three thousand years old. Those of the New Testament floated about in the hands of private, and sometimes partisan and bitterly interested persons and churches for generations. They were copied widely, and copyists may make mistakes. They may do it through inadvertence, or they may purposely alter. Comments on the margin may get incorporated in the text.

"And then, in no single case, have you

an original manuscript. The oldest you have are no nearer the events they record than we are to the time of Copernicus or Luther. The one that ranks highest, the Sinaitic, was written about the year 350. Thus the time of its writing is farther away from Christ than we are from Shakespeare, by as much as a hundred years. And when you remember the discrepancies between, and the disputes over, the different copies of his poems, — and this is an age of printing, — we may gain some idea of the possibility of departure from the earliest, in some of the later copies of the New Testament books.

"And further, when you remember that it has been gravely discussed whether Shakespeare and Lord Bacon were not identical, you may partly understand the doubts that sometimes cloud the most notorious historical facts."

But, we reply, —

2. These books are infallibly inspired, and so, of course, would be infallibly preserved for us by an overruling Providence. How much will our critic allow us on this score ?

The latter point, the infallible preservation, he will hardly deign to answer. He will say, " That is all pure assumption, invented in order to a consistent carrying out of your doctrine of Inspiration."

Of the infallible Inspiration, he will say hardly less severe things. " First, the Bible nowhere makes any claim to infallibility. Secondly, if some one writer does make claim to speak as from God, his claim covers no one else, since nowhere does the Bible pretend to be one complete book. Thirdly, if it did claim to be one book, and infallible, you would even then need an infallible list of what the infallible books are ; and also, an infallible preservation of manuscripts, or infallible copyists; to none of which can you make any respectable pretension. Fourthly, the New Testament writers quote the Old loosely, and even inaccurately, which they would not be justified in doing. if verbal accuracy were of any great importance. Fifthly, there are great discrepancies and contradictions in the accounts of transactions, in details of history, in names, in genealogies, in numbers, and in science. Sixthly, the doubts concerning the authenticity of many of the Biblical books militate against their infallibility. And seventhly, the Apostles were mistaken on some points, as, for example, concerning the bodily advent of Christ in their generation. And also, they were in open opposition on some, as, for example, concerning the attitude of the Church toward the Gentiles. And if they mistook here, why not elsewhere?"

But again we say,—

3. The fulfillment of prophecy is a sure prop to uphold Christianity.

And again the critic makes answer: "Before relying much on prophecy, let your Christian scholarship first come to some sort of an agreement as to what the prophets mean, and to what they allude. As yet, many of them are hardly more than dissected pictures with which children play. The different theorizers put them together to make whatever picture the fancy, the theory, or the prejudice of each one determines.

"Not only is there little agreement about many of the Old Testament prophecies, but concerning the most modern of all; the Apocalypse of John, there are almost as many theories as there are commentators. And the antagonistic branches of Christendom are sure that the worst constructions and denunciations were meant for each other; so that the Protestant sees Rome in the Scarlet Woman and the Man of Sin; and the Romanist equally sees Luther and Protestantism.

" No very staunch argument can be built on the fulfillment of prophecy, until you can find out what it means, and when it may be regarded as fulfilled."

4. At any rate there are the miracles, we reply. How can they be disregarded ? And again comes the opponent's answer : " First, rarely, if ever, does the Christ Himself offer them in evidence of his claims or teachings, which he could hardly have failed to do, had He considered them of special importance in that direction. Secondly, nowhere do the Apostles and first preachers of Christianity make any such use of them. And they would have availed little if they had ; for the people of those times had so little idea of law or nature, that miracles meant but little. And any common juggler could astonish them as effectually as could the Christ. Thirdly, there is as much exter-

nal proof for the miracles of the time of
Augustine as for those of the apostolic
age; and yet they are rejected by common consent. Fourthly, the miracles to-
day, so far from being a support to Christianity, are a burden and a hindrance, a
difficulty to be met and explained. They
do not support the Christ so much as He
supports them. Did they cluster about
any other character of history they would
be unhesitatingly rejected. Fifthly, a miracle never did, and never can substantiate
a moral truth. Should a teacher appear
now and work miracles in support of
teachings that contravened our moral
sense, it would be our duty to reject him.
For it would be more reasonable to regard
him as an impostor than to suppose our
God-given moral intuitions were false."

In setting forth the difficulties connected with these points of proof, it will
be seen that I have let the outside critic
have his own way. And I have done

this purposely. For if you are to argue with a man, you must have some common starting place. And in attempting to convince an opponent, you must begin at some point which he will allow. It will not do to have some reason for belief in your own heart, of which your opponent can necessarily know nothing, and then go on to condemn him for not being convinced by arguments. that never did, and never could, convince yourself. I suppose none of us ever became Christians under the power of a persuasion drawn from miracles, or prophecy, or inspiration. Generally we have inherited our Christianity. It is not the worse for that, and it could hardly be otherwise. But is it quite fair to demand that others submit for the sake of reasons that have not and could not have produced submission in ourselves?

What are the steps of the proof we have been reviewing, as they appear to those outside the Christian ranks ? Let the critic again say: "No one of your points is of any value until you have made an assumption that includes them all. In order that the argument from miracles or prophecy should be of any worth, you must assume an infallible inspiration. And in order that the infallibility of inspiration should be substantiated, you must assume an infallible transmission of records, and the authenticity of much which can never be proved."

That these are weak points in an argument with doubters is but too apparent. That ministers and churches are partly conscious of their weakness, appears in the suspicious and unreasonable jealousy of those who are accustomed to rely upon them. In no ministerial association with which I have ever been acquainted, would it be possible to conduct a calm and judicial discussion of questions like these. He who should plead for such a discussion would be laying himself liable to suspicion of heresy. And yet such suspicion is unreasonable and unchristian. If the claimed facts are true, the jealousy of question is unreasonable: if not true, it is unchristian and unjust.

However irrefragable these proofs may appear to one already convinced on other grounds, it is clear that we cannot gain through them the conviction of the world. And, since they are historic in their nature, and have their root in a past that is ever becoming more and more distant, it can hardly be but that they will progressively weaken and lose force. It is then a most serious question, as to whether he is a friend to Christianity who seeks to identify any of these doubtful accessories with Christianity itself. The preacher or writer who takes the position that the strict accuracy of every part of the Bible

must be maintained, or else Christianity
is lost, may be a very zealous man ; but
it may fairly be questioned as to whether
his judiciousness is equal to his zeal. And
the same holds true of any other such
non-essential identification.

Just so long as the faith of Christendom
rests on these externals of Christianity,
it is subject to perpetual threat, and liable to overthrow. Every quibbler can
propose difficulties that cannot be answered. Every critic can pick flaws that
no one can mend or cover up. Unbelief
will always be imminent; and the accepted mode of defense will continue to
be what it so largely is now, namely, the
method of the young partridge or ostrich
— sticking the head under a leaf, or into
the sand.

To say that Christianity needs, as supports, and must have, what manifestly God
has not given us, — that is, absolutely un-
questionable historic proof, — is only to

impeach either the wisdom or the goodness of God. It is safer to assume that He has given us all we really need. And if He has, we only weaken our cause by saying we ought to have more; or by saying it is not safe to look publicly into the real state of affairs. If they will not bear looking into, it is because they are unsound. If they are unsound, the world ought to know it.

CHAPTER III.

THE INDEPENDENCE OF CHRISTIANITY.

IT were hardly unjust to declare that the evidential foundations of Christianity are — as ordinarily presented — very much in the condition of the ancient, popular foundations of the earth. First there was the tortoise, and then the rock, and below that something else, and beneath, a lower something still, and so on to the bottom. And yet the thought could find no bottom, because there was no bottom to find. The intelligence and science of the world at last discovered that the earth needed no foundation, but swung and moved free and self-poised, hung on nothing but the will of her omnipotent Creator.

This lesson needs to be learned concerning Christianity. The old, and still ordinary method of evidence, of which Paley is the prominent example, is of very little use to one who does not already believe; and he does not need it. It first assumes something that can never be proved, as its tortoise, and then begins its descent toward the first and foundation stone. But the deeper the descent the more confused the chaos. And the last stone the ever receding space forbids to find.

There needs then, if possible, to be found a resting-place for belief that is independent, that earthquakes of doubt cannot shake, that cannot grow old, that will not weaken, but will rather increase in force as the years advance. Is there any such basis? I think there is: and that it is to be found in the ability of Christianity to hang and move self-poised.

Trust it to God and its self-balancing power, and see if it will not ride at ease as gracefully as ever did planet in its ether. And when it is thus swung and poised, the critics may seek to dig away its foundations with about as brilliant a prospect of success as might a party of sappers and miners go down to China with the purpose of exploding the corner-stone of the earth.

As our starting-point, then, let us take only the facts and the book, — the world as it is, and the Bible, — and we will assume nothing as to where they came from, or how they came to be as they are.

Leaving them now for a little, let us come back to them through an illustration. Suppose I have never seen or heard of a sewing-machine. I have no idea of its parts, of its construction, or its use. But — no matter how — after a time I come into possession of one. It is not set up, however, nor even put together. I have the wheels, and bands, and arms, and the cloth-plate, and the shuttle, and the needles, and the treadle, — in short, all the parts which compose it. But not being a machinist, and never having seen one, I do not know how to put the parts together, nor what they are all for. So I throw them into a box, and put them away. By and by there comes to me through the mail a pamphlet. The postmark is dim, and I cannot make it out. It has no name on it, either of author or sender. I look it curiously through, and find it full of cuts and explanatory letterpress. And as I turn over the leaves, I am struck by the resemblance of some of the plates to some of the parts of the almost forgotten and useless machine. I look more closely and find that it is a guide for the setting up and running of something it calls a sewing-machine. I get out and open the old box, and compare the pieces and the book, and following carefully its instructions, I find it all goes accurately together. I thread the needle, and taking a piece of cloth, I find that it works precisely as the book said it would.

Now I care not where the machine came from, and I care not where the book came from. I may not know who wrote the book, or even as much as that the inventor of the machine ever heard of him, or his writing. The letter-press of the pamphlet may be mixed up with fables, and wild mechanical theories and speculations. The cuts may be from wood, and poorly executed. But, whatever else is true, this much I know is true, namely, that the idea of him who made the machine, and the idea of him who made the book, are identical. In that wherein it pretends to be a guide — that is, in putting together and running the machine — it is an accurate guide-book; and being thus true for the ends for which it was made, it is, for such ends, an absolute authority. No conceivable thing could add to this authority. If it could be proved that the inventor of the machine wrote the book with his own hands, and that all his theories and speculations were correct, and that it was free from mistake throughout, even to the grammar and punctuation, it would not add to its essential truthfulness or binding authority one iota. It works. It stands trial. It does what it claims to do. And that is all we ask or want.

Now suppose somebody should go to picking flaws in its spelling, or grammar, or outside theories, or chronological calculations, or obscurities of style, or the taste of some anecdote that fills a vacant spot, or the credibility of some wonder related, or because a stray leaf from an old almanac had got bound up in it; suppose, for such reasons, he should counsel throwing it away, and trusting to luck to get the machine together. Would you not call him a fool, or else think he were jesting?

Or suppose, on the other hand, that some one who deeply felt the need of it, and who feared it might be thrown away on account of the flaws, should undertake to sanctify and defend all the points objected to : suppose he should even plant himself on the assertion, that, if one of the flaws were thrown away, the whole thing had got to go by the board with it,— would he be any less foolish than the other?

Essentially, and for the purpose for which it was made, it is true and infallible, as proved by trial. Who wants any more?

Come back now to the book and the world, and see if we have not for Christianity an argument equally simple and irrefragable.

Here is a disordered, or incomplete humanity. For our present purpose, I care not when or how it came so, nor in what the disorder consists. I have no word to say of Adam or Eve or serpent. It is a fact, staring every observer in the face, that humanity is disordered. We have only the separate and unjointed parts of a complete humanity. The individual is disordered. The family is disordered. Society is disordered. States are disordered. The great company of nations jar, and do not fit, nor work together.

Here also is a book. For our present purpose, I care not when, nor where, nor how, nor by whom it was composed. Look into it. It contains pictures of the present condition of humanity. It tells how to put the parts together, and make it complete. Try it by this test, and it is infallible. On its principle, and on that alone, — the principle of love, — you can build up a perfect man, a perfect family, a perfect society, a perfect state, a perfect world. Just so far as the world has progressed, it is toward the realization of this idea. Carry it out completely, and the result will be perfection.

Now somebody goes to picking flaws in the book. He questions its chronology: he suspects its historical accuracy; he doubts some of its alleged marvels; he impugns some of its theories of man, or of science. It is as profitable, and as relevant to the question, as spitting at the moon.

Or somebody else says, that in order to have any benefit of it whatever, you must hold and defend the absolute accuracy of every book, of every chapter, of every verse, and he calls by hard names those who cannot agree with him. Such a course is at the least an unwarranted assumption. Neither the book, nor Christianity, nor reason asks it. Both sides build on folly.

In bringing out the argument, we can afford to disregard the positions of both. It is enough that taking the central principle of the book for a guide, you can put together and "run" humanity perfectly.

This one fact proves conclusively that the essential idea that is embodied in humanity, and the essential idea of the book, are the same. In that wherein it pretends to be a guide — that is, in putting together and building up humanity — it is an accurate guide-book, and being thus true for the ends for which it was made, it is, for such ends, an absolute authority. No conceivable thing could add to this authority. If it could be proved that the maker of humanity wrote the book with his own hands, and dropped it down from the sky, and that all its theories and statements were absolutely and literally accurate, it would not add to its essential truthfulness or binding authority one iota. Nothing can be higher authority than visible truth ; and all truth, no matter through what channels, nor mixed with how much so ever sediment, must have come from the one source of all truth.

What now are the advantages of this defense of Christianity? Many, every way. And this, for short; it gives the skeptic all he asks, and beats him then. It makes Christianity as independent as a star in its orbit. It hangs self-poised, and proves itself by shining. Criticism is completely flanked, and Christianity is essentially true in spite of it.

To particularize. It is independent of geological criticism. "Genesis and Geology" may fight it out to suit themselves. It is independent of chronology. Bishop Colenso may cipher away to his heart's content.

It is independent of disputed questions in prophecy. Daniel may or may not have been written by one author, and nobody tremble. It is independent of gospel criticism or authorship. John may or may not have written John. Strauss and Renan may work as they will over the life and character of Jesus. It matters not. It is independent of the question of authenticity of books. Who wrote them, or when, or where, touches not the force of the argument in the least.

It is independent of any theory of inspiration. Call it verbal, plenary, or what not, and so the name suits your fancy, it is all one to me. The simple fact, that the central principle of the Bible holds the key to the perfection of humanity, is absolute proof that they belong together, and that their controlling ideas are identical. If one came from God, so must the other have come.

And not only is this proof independent of Biblical criticism ; it has other advantages not less valuable.

It appeals to all men alike. To understand it, and feel its force, requires no great culture, nor prolonged study. Very few persons are fitted to judge whether the ordinary proofs are worth anything or not.

It is of present force, and cannot be endangered by any rear attack. Not depending for its cogency on any questionable historic statement, historical criticism cannot undermine it.

The process of time, so far from diminishing or weakening its force, can only make it continually stronger and stronger. For as humanity grows more and more into its likeness, their relationship to each other, and the mutual support they render, will be more and more apparent.

And then, as for the ordinary arguments, they remain just where they were before. They are just as valuable, and of equal force. But all fear concerning their fate is taken away. Critics will not think they've overthrown the citadel of Christianity when they have only captured an insignificant earth-work. The different bodies of Christendom need not waste their strength and time in hunting up each other's heresies. And scholars may calmly pursue their investigations after fact, with no more bias than has the seeker after scientific truth. And because some one finds a new truth, or discovers the falsity of what was supposed true, he need not hereafter be called hard names. In a word, all these questions may be turned over to the calm and impartial inquiry of trained and competent investigators. And we may ask of them, not that they support systems, but only that they report truth.

Any one of these points were an immense gain. Take them all together, and the advantages are incalculable. Christianity stands forth the child of Him who is the father of humanity, and her own beauty and power attest her divine.

———•———

CHAPTER I.

TO NEW THEORIZERS.

THE age is one of invention and improvement. Completer theories, better methods, more efficient machines, these are sought in all directions. And it is not to be expected that theology, morality, or manhood should escape any more than politics and mechanics. And no lover of truth would have them escape. The things that are true can only be purged by search and trial; and the things that are false no friend of man would have preserved. Let Christianity, then, take its chances with the rest.

The present object, therefore, is not to

warn thinkers and critics and theorizers off the orthodox premises. Rather let all fences be thrown down, and make search who will. Only to suggest queries to the student does this chapter come.

Science may be regarded as having settled the methods of investigation for this generation at the least. And he who simply speculates may succeed in amusing himself and possibly other people; but he will hardly succeed in convincing. All advance must be in accord with facts and settled principles. All improvements in manhood and religion must be looked for on this basis. And he who flippantly casts aside the facts of Christianity will be as much disregarded by the earnest lookers for truth, as he who blinks facts in any other field.

In the light then of our past discussion, I wish to suggest some thoughts to new theorizers on these subjects. And —

1. Is not the ideal of manhood that

has been set forth the true one? — that is, is it not in accord with the facts of history, and the observed principles of human nature? and can anything higher be imagined? and is it not true that it is, as set forth, the true Christian ideal, and that towards which Christianity has been continually working?

If this be so, the attempt to find anything better must necessarily be a failure. And that which the world settles on at last, in the time of its "perfect equilibrium," must be, no matter what name you give it, essentially Christian.

2. Is it not true that all the world's so-far progress is in the direction of real, practical Christianity? No matter how, or when, or where achieved, whether through science or philosophy, whether by heathen or Christian, all real advance has been towards the realization of essentially Christian principles. Whatever is recognized as beautiful or true in Veda or

Avesta, in the Classics of Confucius or the Koran, in Plato's "Republic," in Sidney's "Arcadia," in all the world's dreaming and thinking and hoping, is just that wherein they each chime in with the central principle of Christianity.

The front rank of the world's best and highest life is just that which is nearest true Christianity. And unless some way be found by which man can outgrow his own highest ideal, it is impossible to conceive of his leaving Christianity behind.

3. Since these things are so, does it not follow that all thought and time and effort spent in trying to find something better, is just so much taken from the true welfare of man? Not that science and philosophy should be discouraged; for these are but parts of, and ministers to, Christianity. But if Christianity be accordant with the foundation principles of human nature, then nothing beyond it, or higher than it, or better than it, can

exist, save in somebody's dreams. And as each man owes his utmost to his fellows, he should give himself to the advance and up-lifting of the world.

This may not always be done most successfully by what is called religious work. It will be by each man's seeking to develop the pure truth and right in his own department of work or study. For the true Christianity, which is the true manhood, is inclusive of all things that are true and right. Thus every right work becomes religious, and enters into the grand plan of the finished world.

4. Are not the faults found with Christianity those of accident or accretion, and not of essence? A careful separation of what can be reasonably substantiated from speculations and assumptions and the influences of outside religions, philosophies, and civilizations, will reveal the fact that the most of those things which the enlightened reason and conscience of the

age are disposed to reject, are really no essential parts of Christianity at all. The most of these we can dispense with as profitably as David did with the armor of Saul.

The artists did not attempt to paint a new and better portrait of Dante; but when the original was discovered under the whitewash on the wall of the larder of the jail that had once been a palace, the loving skill of the world was employed to uncover and restore it. Such is the work needed to be done for Christianity. The accretions and misconceptions and superstitions of the ages need only to be removed, and the fair face of Christian truth will shine out to captivate and charm the world. Its own uncovered beauty is its best defense.

5. Since Christianity, in its essential idea, is identical with the perfection of humanity, it is impossible that any true science or philosophy should be opposed

to it. Misconceptions of Christianity, and misconceptions of truth in science and philosophy, may be antagonistic; but their antagonisms are necessarily in their departures from truth. True Christianity will find room for, and include all truth of whatever kind, and from whatever source. Just as all the light of the earth is from the sun, whether it come through candle, or gas, or wood, or coal, or diamond, so all the truth of the world is Christian truth, no matter through what medium it may shine. The truths of Spencer, and Darwin, and Comte, and Spinoza, and Plato, and Confucius, and Sakya Muni, are Christian truths. If Christianity be the all-inclusive science of manhood, in all its departments, then whatever is essential to the growth of manhood — *i. e.*, all truth, is a part of it. If this be not true, then Christianity did not come from God. If God made man, and if Christianity is seen to be the correlate of the perfect humanity, then this deduction follows of necessity.

6. That other systems of religion and philosophy embrace many common truths of Christianity is only what ought to be expected. And indeed, so far from this fact's making at all against Christianity, it would be enough to disprove it were it not true.

Christianity claims to come from the author of man. Its essential principles then are, and can be, nothing new. They underlie and characterize human nature. They must be synonymous with all truth. If there is anything outside of it, it cannot be coextensive with manhood. When the Copernican system of the universe gained the assent of the world, it was not by creating any new facts. Neither did it do it by rejecting old facts. It only revealed the central organific principle around which all the old facts ranged themselves in a complete harmony of truth. It took up into, and included in itself, all the old truths, and assigned them their place. Its claim on men's acceptance was that it could do this. And so Christianity. It is not built upon the annihilation of other religions. So far as they are true, it includes them all in itself. It harmonizes and arranges. Its claim on men is that it can present a scheme of truth and life that adopts all old and outside truth, and becomes a centre and principle of crystallization. It is the theory that makes itself the solution of all the facts.

CHAPTER II.

TO THE CHURCHES.

SINCE Christianity is the Science of Manhood, and the true religion and the true manhood are identical, it necessarily follows, that the one only work of the Church is to build men. No matter what it may be or do, if it fail in this, it is a total failure. No matter what it may be or do, if it succeed in this, it is God's Church, and a success. It must use means to this end: but the means are of value only in relation to this end. It may love and defend its ways and institutions: but only in so far as it finds them of practical utility in this direction. For the end is divine, being the one great work of God on earth: and the means are only as the sculptor's tools, — good or bad according as they help transform the shapeless block into the image of beauty.

Then, 2. Here is a test by which to try all methods and instruments.

It is not the chief work of the Church to maintain the integrity of its creed. That man is more likely to live rightly whose creed is right. But the creed is a means and not an end, and so of no sort of value in itself. Take the men away, and the creed might go up or down, and no one care. It is of worth then only as it is a vehicle of life and power. A creed is related to a church as the aqueducts, pipes, and water-works are related to a great city. The authorities keep them in repair and perfect order, not for their own sakes, but for what may run through them, to cleanse and keep alive the people. Many churches are as a city which keeps all these in order, but bestows no care on the source of supply. It may be urged, with a show of reason, that the pipes and ducts are absolutely essential, and that the city would die without them. But better that an uncovered and muddy rill should bring them some drops of the life-giving water than that the most splendid apparatus should be maintained and still be dry.

Methods of church government must stand or fall by the same test. That is the best form of order which tends most directly to bring out and develop the complete manhood of the individual, and at the same time to stimulate the sense of mutual dependence and brotherhood.

·Ordinances and forms of service, also, are made for man, and not man for them. It is natural for men to become attached to those ways that are connected with their childhood, or which have about them the odor of antiquity; and these are good reasons for keeping them, provided there are none better for change.

But what is good for the times and the circumstances is that, and that alone, which can give to any of these things their authority. Methods, hours, times, places, and numbers of church service must vary perpetually in accordance with this law; and nothing is of authority which does not prove itself by results.

Sacred days and festivals must come up to this bar for judgment. From it even the Lord's day is not free. Jesus tells us that it was made for man, and not man for it. ˙Any use of it then that hinders the development of manhood is a breaking of it; any use that helps man is its keeping. Questions concerning open or closed libraries and reading rooms, riding, visiting, concerts, and all other matters whatsoever find here their solution.

Orders of the ministry, priesthood, successions, sacraments, robes, altars, candles, churches, chapels; styles of architecture, — whatsoever in any way pertains to the Church is good or bad according to its observed effect on the Church's one work — making men.

3. What is heresy then? Any teaching that hinders the making of manhood. And nothing whatever is essential to orthodoxy that is not essential to this. If there be good reason to suppose that a person is in heart and life loyal to the Christ, no church has any right to refuse its fellowship and help, any more than the United States Consul at Liverpool may, on some private grounds, refuse to recognize the citizenship of a born American. The Church is but the servant of those who are servants of the Church's Lord.

Exclusiveness, or uncharitableness, is a greater heresy then than any intellectual error that does not keep a person away from God. Bigotry and partisanship are worse heresies than mistakes of the head.

No doctrine is fundamental that is not absolutely essential to character.

The worst heresy then is that which misrepresents God, gives men wrong conceptions of his character and relationship toward them, and thus hinders the reconciliation that God seeks in the Christ.

4. In the light of the true church work appears the great evil of sectarian feuds and jealousies. Sects there will, and perhaps must be, because no man's brain and heart are comprehensive enough to include the whole of truth. It is right to love one's own peculiar beliefs and ways, just as it is right to love one's own regiment and regimental flag. But as he who puts his regiment before the army and the cause is a traitor to the very government for which all the regiments exist, so he who puts his sect before the work of saving men is false to God and truth. The churches exist for the sake of the men who need them. They for-

feit their right to live at all then when they cease living for men, and begin to live for themselves.

Let the little churches that waste their strength in rival struggles for existence learn this lesson.

5. God seeks the saving of men, *i. e.* the building up of the true manhood. Putting anything else before that is impiety toward Him.

6. More than all things else, men need this saving, *i. e.*, the being brought into the true manhood. Putting anything else before that is inhuman.

7. This principle must determine the Church's attitude toward amusements.

The true manhood means the recognition, development, and regulation of all that is a real part of man. The play-element in man is universal. It follows that God did not make man, that He made him wrongly, or that this play-element is right. That it often runs into excess is only what every other part of manhood does. And if this condemns one, it condemns all. If Christianity cannot control and regulate, but must seek to kill out and annihilate it, it is only a confession that it is incompetent to the task it has undertaken, — that is, the building up of a full, complete, regulated manhood.

The Church has no commission from God to exterminate anything that God has made. It is to develop, control, regulate, and complete. However often it fail, or whether the task be long or short, touches not the question at all. It must do it, or confess failure.

8. The Church should beware, in its organizations, teachings, methods, influences, that it do not identify with Christanity, in the minds of men, this, that, or another thing, that is not essential to Christianity, and thus secure its own rejection. Many are standing without

the churches to-day, who would be in it, but for this one thing.

9. If then the Church will not lose her power, and fall behind the age, let her address herself to this one thing, the making over into God's image of men.

This is the one thing the world needs, and that toward which all true and intelligent men are striving. The Church has many rival organizations and agencies in this work. Many are the theories and methods that are on trial. Science, Philosophy, Philanthropy, Societies, Books, Newspapers, Lectures, — all these, as well as churches and preachers, are in the field. Some are claiming a preëminence, and that the work of the Church is well-nigh past. Written or preached assertions of vigor and capacity are not enough. That one will succeed which succeeds. That one will be ahead which leads. That is God's agent which does his work. That has most divinity and authority in it which manifests in work and accomplishment the most of God's love and power. Past achievements and past claims are good for the past, but not for the present.

Let the churches then drop all other things and prove their power to build up the true manhood, and they will then be seen to be in the line of God's advance up the ages, and nothing can ever overthrow them, or leave them behind.

12

CHAPTER III.

1. CHRISTIANITY is true to the idea of humanity. This one fact, in spite of any and everything else, proves its absolute and binding truth. That, practically applied, it will produce a perfect humanity, proves that it is in accord with the idea or plan after which man was made, or is developing, and the living out of which will constitute his perfection. Advancing Christianity is advancing man. Lifting up Christianity is lifting up man. Degrading Christianity is degrading man. Distorting it is distorting man. Standing in the way of its progress is hindering man.

2. Estimate then the probable gain of neglecting Christianity in the hope of

finding something better. Its ideal is absolute perfection; and so far as men will submit to it they are transformed into its likeness. Surely nothing better than this can be found: and all things are good only in so far as they approach it.

3. Judge the value of criticisms on the churches, and the imperfections of Christians. It is fair that a person be judged on the basis of the claims he makes. But no Christian claims perfection by joining the Church. He professes to take upon himself no new obligations. He thereby declares himself a disciple, a learner, of the Christ. He only acknowledges obligations that were always binding, and that now he begins to discharge. A church is only a band of fallible persons organized to help each other and the world into the Christian life. And profession is no more a declaration of sainthood, than enlistment in the army is a profession of perfect bravery and heroism.

Let the Church then be judged by its claims.

A Christian is only in process in this life. You would not judge a ship by the lumber in the ship yard, or the timbers half up. If you wish to criticise, look either at the model in the office of the master-builder, or else go out on the broad sea where the finished ships are sailing. The Christian only asks the same fairness in the matter of judging him.

4. The discussion in which we have been engaged may also teach the value of the shallow and flippant criticisms of the Christian Scriptures that are so common. They may hold as against certain claims that are made on their behalf by certain men. But as against their real value and right use they are utterly foolish and futile. As already brought out, their central and controlling idea contains the germ of a perfect humanity.

They constitute a complete guide-book toward the " perfect day." Criticism of parts, or shallow wit at the expense of what may appear strange or incredible, touches not this great fact at all. It is therefore only a display of ignorance or vulgarity.

5. The misrepresentations of Christianity, on the part of Christians, Christian ministers, or churches, have nothing to do with the propriety or duty of your becoming at once practical Christians. There are such misrepresentations in teaching, in institutions, in living. But they do not militate against the true, any more than false science, philosophy, or mechanics, makes it reasonable to reject whatever bears their names.

6. Becoming a Christian takes away nothing worth keeping. It only forbids perversion and excess. It commands the right development and use of body, heart, mind, and spirit. Whatever is right, *i. e.*

does not transgress the laws of your being, it allows. Whatever is wrong it forbids; and a true and enlightened selfishness would do that.

Christianity is not the religion of repression and narrowness and bigotry, but of the largest, widest, fullest life.

And since happiness is the result of the healthy play and satisfaction of the largest number of man's passions, faculties, and powers, he who is built and who lives on the Christian plan will be the happiest man. The complete manhood in complete exercise will produce the most of enjoyment; just as a violin, perfectly kept and tuned, will give out the most and the richest music.

7. If Christianity is really the law of human life, then it follows necessarily that breaking it is death. This is the true fear-element in religion.

Individual being supposes and necessitates those limitations that hem in and constitute the individuality. To break through these limitations is to destroy the individual. A steam-engine is such only by its conformity to the laws of its structure. A river is a river only by keeping within its banks. A man is a man only by obeying the laws of manhood. The physical being dies if its laws are persistently disregarded. It is only common sense that the same should hold true of the moral and religious nature.

8. There is great gain in beginning at once to be a Christian. Beside the time lost that might have been given to God and man, there is the matter of personal development.

The old notion that all the saved are alike by virtue of getting into a city, the entrance to which constitutes salvation, is well-nigh exploded, and it ought completely to be. Death is a line. He who steps over finds himself on that side what he was on this, and his heaven is limited by his capacity. Just as in this life two persons may not get the same amount of pleasure from one of Beethoven's Symphonies, so in heaven, one person may find a thousand times more than another, because of developed capacity and fitness to receive. He who stands on the border-land the truest in service, and the most highly developed, will be the best fitted to enter in and possess the glory, and happiness, and beauty.

9. Since then Christianity is the law of human perfection, any lack of allegiance to it is high treason against man. The life of one is inextricably intertwined with the other. Not a selfish thought is entertained, or a selfish wish harbored, but is a wrong against man. Not a selfish pleasure is tasted, or a selfish scheme pursued, but is just so much obstruction placed across the pathway of human progress. This one word, love, has in it the cure for every possible, namable human

ill. So long then as any one delays or declines to utter it, he refuses to do his part toward the consummation of that for which the world longs, and sighs, and prays, and struggles.

Suppose that, during the late fearful fire in Boston, there had been one engine house in the city that contained machinery and appliances capable of immediately stopping the flames. And suppose that some person had and kept the key. While granite walls are crumbling, and fortunes are shriveling in the heat; while men and women and children are struggling to save themselves or their goods; while homes are being ruined; while strong men strive, and women weep, the possessor of the key, the knowledge of which might end it all, goes lounging about whistling or humming a tune, with his hands in his pockets. Is there any plummet of language capable of sinking so low as to measure the depth of his guilt? Not a heart-pang, nor a falling tear; not a broken home, nor a ruined fortune; not a lost dollar, nor a lost life, but would equally and justly be chargeable on him. And if the number of persons holding keys were a hundred or a thousand, instead of one, the principle would be the same.

This is but a fair illustration of the case we have in hand. Each man holds in his hand the key to the deliverance from all evil of the sphere which he occupies and controls. Only let each one accept and live out the Christ ideal, and evil would disappear as the mist flees the valleys and hill-sides when the sun is up.

The first and pressing duty then of every man is to become a practical Christian. You have no right to delay it an hour; for nothing else can be so important. As an individual, for the sake of your own development and highest self-interest, you are bound to the duty of being a Christian. For the sake of the disordered and broken family life of the world, and by the importance of perfected households, you are bound to be a Christian. For the sake of society, and that its infinite wrongs and wounds may be healed, you are bound to be a Christian. Your first political duty, that national and international relations may be perfected, and that the dawn of the world's future morning may hasten the rising of its star, is to become a Christian. No reason is valid against, and every voice of heaven and earth combines in the one ceaseless and urgent utterance. It is your first great duty to become a Christian.